Sophie Steps Up

JUL 2012 CH

Other books in the growing Faithgirlz!™ library

The Faithgirlz!™ Bible
NIV Faithgirlz!™ Backpack Bible
My Faithgirlz!™ Journal

The Sophie Series

Sophie's World (Book One)
Sophie's Secret (Book Two)
Sophie Under Pressure (Book Three)
Sophie's First Dance (Book Five)
Sophie's Stormy Summer (Book Six)
Sophie's Friendship Fiasco (Book Seven)
Sophie and the New Girl (Book Eight)
Sophie Flakes Out (Book Nine)
Sophie Loves Jimmy (Book Ten)
Sophie's Drama (Book Eleven)
Sophie Gets Real (Book Twelve)

Nonfiction

Body Talk
Beauty Lab
Everybody Tells Me to Be Myself but I Don't Know Who I Am
Girl Politics

Check out www.faithgirlz.com

SOPHIE
Steps Up

4

Previously titled Sophie's Irish Showdown

Nancy Rue

ZONDERVAN.com/
AUTHORTRACKER
follow your favorite authors

ZONDERKIDZ

Sophie Steps Up
Previously titled *Sophie's Irish Showdown*
Copyright © 2005, 2009 by Nancy Rue

Requests for information should be addressed to:

Zondervan, *Grand Rapids, Michigan* 49530

Library of Congress Cataloging-in-Publication Data

Rue, Nancy N.
    [Sophie's Irish showdown]
    Sophie Steps Up / Nancy Rue.
       p. cm. — (Sophie series ; bk. 4) (Faithgirlz!)
    Summary: As the Corn Flakes and a new student from Ireland prepare for a "Performance Showcase," tempers flare and Sophie retreats to her imagination again, but a Bible story recommended by Dr. Peter helps her pull the group together.
    ISBN 978-0-310-71841-3 (softcover)
     [1. Talent shows—Fiction. 2. Friendship—Fiction. 3. Irish Americans—Fiction. 4. Orphans—Fiction. 5. Schools—Fiction. 6. Imagination—Fiction. 7. Christian life—Fiction. 8. Virginia—Fiction.] I. Title.
    PZ7.R88515Sjr 2009
    [Fic]—dc22   2008047113

Published in association with the literary agency of Alive Communications, Inc., 7680 Goddard Street, Suite 200, Colorado Springs, CO 80920. www.alivecommunucations.com

Zonderkidz is a trademark of Zondervan.

Interior art direction and design: Sarah Molegraaf
Cover illustrator: Steve James
Interior design and composition: Carlos Estrada and Sherri L. Hoffman

Printed in the United States of America

---

09 10 11 12 13 14 15 16 • 24 23 22 21 20 19 18 17 16 15 14 13 12 11 10 9 8 7 6 5 4 3 2 1

So we fix our eyes not on what is seen,
but on what is unseen.
For what is seen is temporary,
but what is unseen is eternal.

—2 Corinthians 4:18

One

Sophie LaCroix could not believe what she had just heard.

There was no way Miss Blythe had just announced that the sixth-grade class was going to get to do a performance showcase — on the stage — on a Saturday night — in front of a REAL AUDIENCE. And that the top three performing groups would each get a prize.

In Sophie's world, dreams like THAT just didn't come true every day.

Sophie's best friend, Fiona, grabbed her hand and squeezed it until Sophie's fingers looked like red lipsticks.

"Do you think she'll let us pick our own groups?" Kitty whispered on Sophie's other side. Her robin's-egg-blue eyes were nearly bulging, the way they always did when she was nervous. Which was a lot.

"She would be nonsensical not to," Fiona whispered back. "We're the Corn Flakes."

"So?" That came from their other friend, Maggie, whose voice thudded across the table they shared. "Teachers don't care about that."

Sophie looked at Miss Blythe, who had her back to them, writing dates and times and requirements on the board with squeaky chalk. She was their arts teacher, and Sophie had often thought she couldn't have been anything else.

Miss Blythe was tall and wore long skirts and bracelets that bounced with bright-colored charms. She swayed like a new tree when she walked, the strands of her waist-length blonde hair streaming down her back as if they were rays of sunlight. With her long fingers constantly punctuating her sentences in the air, Sophie had a hard time imagining her as a lawyer or a greeter down at Wal-Mart. And Sophie could imagine just about anything.

Is Miss Blythe the type to let friends—best friends who can't bear to be separated—work together? Sophie thought. *Or would she subject her students to pure torture at the hands of girls like the Corn Pops?* They'd only had arts class for about a month. It was hard to say.

"I can't work with Julia and them!" Kitty was whining. She did that a lot too. "She and B.J. and Anne-Stuart and Willoughby—they would be so mean to me!"

"Yeah, they would torture you," Maggie said in her usual flat, factual voice. "Any of us."

Sophie could tell by the way Kitty was whimpering that none of that was making her feel any better. It wasn't doing much for Sophie either, for that matter. She shook her acorn-colored hair off her shoulders and adjusted her glasses as she leaned into the table. The rest of the Corn Flakes leaned in with her.

"We just have to pray really hard," she said. "We have to squeeze our eyes shut and whisper to God in our heads."

"That'll look weird," Maggie said. Sophie saw that she was on the point of rolling her very dark eyes. Maggie was Cuban, so everything on her was dark except her extra-white teeth.

"Corn Flakes are weird," Fiona told her. "That's what makes us unique. Close your eyes."

They all did, clutching each other's hands under the table. Just before she shut hers, Sophie saw the Corn Pops clinging to each other too, but she was pretty sure they weren't praying.

In fact, Sophie wondered if the Corn Pops EVER prayed. What they did do, as far as Sophie could tell, was think they were better than everybody else because they had more money than rock stars and could get their way no matter what. "No matter what" included cheating, lying, gossiping, and teasing people about anything they thought was too weird.

And since the Corn Pops considered everything the Corn Flakes did way too weird, Sophie and Maggie and Kitty and Fiona were their favorite targets.

At least we used to be, Sophie thought now. *Until they got in so much trouble for doing bad stuff and blaming it on us.*

It was a little bit of a comfort that the Corn Pops wouldn't dare do anything else to the Corn Flakes, at least not anything they could possibly get caught at. But Sophie knew the Pops had ways of getting away with things that could escape even the really smart teachers. She sure hoped Miss Blythe knew a Pop from a Flake and wouldn't try to mix them together.

It's pretty easy to see the differences, Sophie thought.

The Corn Pops only wanted to be popular—which was why they were Pops—and they would do anything to stay the boss of everybody else in the sixth grade at Great Marsh Elementary, which was where the corn part came from. Sometimes they were so corny in the stuff they did.

Sophie unsquinted her eyes open a little so she could peek at her fellow Flakes. Fiona, with her rich-brown bob that fell over one of her gray eyes. Maggie, so serious and stocky and practical. And Kitty, with her curly ponytail and her little nose that looked like it was made of china.

Corn Flakes are corny too, Sophie thought. *That's what everyone says just because we like to make up stories and make films out of them, and we don't care what anybody else thinks about that.*

Once, back when Kitty was still a Pop, the CPs had said Sophie and Fiona were a couple of "flakes." It was so perfect it had to be their name. After that, the girls who were all into sports were the Wheaties and most of the boys were Fruit Loops. The best part was that all the group names were a secret among the Corn Flakes.

"If everyone is awake, I'll finish explaining the project," Miss Blythe said.

Sophie's brown eyes sprang open, even though she hadn't actually gotten to praying at all. She pulled her elf-like body up as tall as she could in her chair. It wouldn't be good to be caught daydreaming, or Daddy would take her video camera away from her, and Corn Flakes Productions would be no more. That was the deal with her father—stay out of trouble and make nothing less than a B in school and she could keep the camera. Mess up and it was all history.

"I want at least four people to a group," Miss Blythe said. "And I feel very good about letting you choose your own—"

The rest was drowned out by shrieks that bounced off the walls and back again. Even as Sophie was hugging Fiona and hoping Kitty wasn't going to spill off her chair into a puddle of relief, she saw that the Corn Pops were every bit as excited. B.J.—the pudgy-faced one with the swingy blonde hair—was whistling through her teeth. Willoughby, of course, was letting out one of her poodle laughs that could set a person's fillings on edge, and Anne-Stuart was blowing her nose. Anne-Stuart had sinus issues. She was always blowing her nose.

Above it all was the Corn Pop Queen Bee, Julia Cummings, tossing her thick, curly auburn hair back from her face and looking as if she had expected nothing else. After all, she always got what she wanted.

Even as Sophie watched her, Julia turned to meet her eyes. Julia's went into slits, but she wore a smile that looked as if she'd selected it from a rack of grins and stuck it onto her face. Sophie had learned that every one of Julia's smiles had a message to send. This one clearly said, *Thank heaven I didn't get stuck with any of you.*

Sophie smiled back—a real smile. People always told her that her smile was wispy, like a wood fairy's. Sophie didn't know about that—she just knew that right now, it wiped Julia's own grin right off her mouth and replaced it with another message, etched into a sneer:

Don't even think about getting a prize, Sophie LaCroix, because we are so going to win.

"All right—let's settle down," Miss Blythe called out above the din. "Artists are disciplined people—remember that."

She perched on the high stool at the front of the room and began to make periods and commas in the air with her long fingers as she talked.

"Each group must decide on an idea for a performance that is to last no more than ten minutes at the very most."

One of the Wheaties, a softball-playing girl named Harley, poked her arm into the air. "What kinda stuff can we do?" she said. Her group all had their foreheads in twists, Sophie noticed.

"Anything the audience might enjoy," Miss Blythe said. Her eyes took on a dreamy look. "You can sing, dance, do gymnastics, present a poem—"

That got a couple of snickers from some of the Fruit Loops, but Miss Blythe ignored them.

"Think about what gifts and talents the members of your group have and put them together into something fabulous. And remember..." She arched an eyebrow at the class. "You will be graded not only on the performance itself, but also on how organized you are and how well you are able to work together."

Sophie sighed happily. Maggie would be in charge of organization. Maggie, herself, and Fiona would do the thinking. And Kitty would do whatever they wanted her to because she always did.

"We are so going to have the best one," Fiona whispered to them.

"I want you to meet with your groups now," Miss Blythe said, curving a comma with her pinkie finger, "and go to work on coming up with an idea. I need to see it in writing by one week from today. That's next Thursday. If you don't have anything by then, I will assign a poem for your group to present."

"She'll have ours way before next Thursday," Maggie said.

As soon as Miss Blythe punched out the final period with a deep-purple fingernail, Maggie got out the Corn Flakes' purple Treasure Book and the special color-of-the-day gel pen, a shade of pale peach. Fiona got her finger around the section of hair that hung over her eye and twirled it. Sophie recognized that as her creative thinking pose. Sophie's was to tuck her way-skinny legs up under her and gaze at the ceiling.

It was Kitty, however, who spoke first. "Good thing we already know what our talent is. What can we make a film of?"

"Film?"

They all looked up at Miss Blythe, who had stopped beside their table with a swish of her lavender skirt.

"That's what we do," Fiona told her. "We write scripts and make films out of them. They're always educational. We do our research and we have costumes and—"

"I'm impressed," Miss Blythe said. "But you can't make a film for the Sixth Grade Showcase. This has to be a live performance."

Then she looked at the Corn Flakes as if they obviously didn't know what art really was and swept off to visit the Wheaties.

Kitty's voice immediately spiraled up into a whine. "But what do we do if we can't make a film?"

"Not fair," Maggie said.

"I'm gonna go talk to her," Fiona said.

But Sophie shook her head. "We'll think of something else," she said. "I get in trouble when I argue with teachers."

Fiona plucked at her little bunch of a mouth with her fingers. "Let's go around the table and everybody say what their talent is—besides making films."

For a long moment, nobody said anything. Finally Fiona snapped her fingers.

"I used to take ballet," she said.

"When?" Maggie said.

"When I was five. Only my parents had to take me out because the teacher didn't like me. I kept correcting the way she was pronouncing the positions. She was saying everything wrong."

Maggie had the peach pen poised over the blank page. "So Fiona can dance, but I can't."

"Me neither," Sophie said.

Kitty shook her head.

"Next," Maggie said. "I can make costumes, period."

"And you're the best at it," Sophie said. "Whatever we decide to do, you get to make them for us."

Maggie jotted that down and then looked at Kitty.

"Me?" Kitty said. "I can play the piano. Except the only song I know is 'You Ain't Nothin' But a Hound Dog.' My grandma taught me it. She says it's a classic."

"You know my talent," Sophie said. "I imagine things."

"So what are you imagining right now, Soph?" Fiona said.

"Oh no," Kitty whispered suddenly.

Sophie followed with her eyes to where Kitty was pointing. All the Corn Pops were squealing up to Miss Blythe's desk, and Anne-Stuart was waving around a piece of paper, which she floated down in front of Miss B.

"They couldn't have their idea written up already," Maggie said. She glanced at the wall clock. "It's impossible."

Fiona narrowed her eyes into little points. "They probably cheated."

"Class!" Miss Blythe said. She shot her index finger up into an exclamation point. "Julia's group has already come up with a marvelous idea! They are going to perform a dance with costumes. Doesn't that sound fabulous?"

"Fabulous," said some Fruit Loop in a bored voice.

"Okay, Flakes," Fiona hissed between her teeth. "Everybody has to come up with at least one idea by tomorrow morning—even if it's lame."

Maggie wrote that down too.

"I know your idea won't just be average brilliant," Fiona said to Sophie. "Yours will be scathingly brilliant."

"Oh, by the way—"

That was Anne-Stuart's voice, coming out of her always-stuffy nose. "We are going to need one more dancer. If you are interested in being in our spectacular production, see me and we will set up an audition for you."

Sophie pulled her Corn Flakes in around her with a spread of her arms.

"I'm glad none of us can dance," she said. "Because we will always stick together, right?"

They all agreed that they would. Always.

Two

Sophie could hardly keep her mind on math and science in Mrs. Utley's classes that afternoon, and for once it wasn't because she was imagining herself as Antoinette the French heroine, or Dr. Demetria Diggerty the archaeologist, or Astronaut Stella Stratos. All she could think about was what on earth the Corn Flakes were going to do with one under-trained ballerina and a piano player who could only clunk out some old song about a dog.

She was trying to picture how they could get Fiona's talent for using big words in there when she heard Fiona coughing.

That was the signal that Sophie was in danger of being caught flitting into Sophie World instead of multiplying numbers with decimals. When she looked up, Fiona was jerking her head toward the Corn Pops.

They had their math books open, but their pencils were scrawling out the notes they were passing to each other.

Probably more ideas for their "spectacular dance," Sophie thought. *I'm really glad I'm going to see Dr. Peter today. I know he can help.*

Dr. Peter was Sophie's therapist—her sister, Lacie, still said he was her psychiatrist, even though he wasn't—and one of her favorite people in the galaxy. He was the one who had made it so she could have her camera and make better grades and have real friends. If it weren't for him, Sophie knew she would still be thinking Daddy didn't love her as much as he did Lacie and Zeke.

Mama was in front of the school in the Suburban to pick her up after her last class and take her to Hampton, where Dr. Peter had his office. As usual, Sophie's five-year-old brother, Zeke, was in the backseat yacking his head off.

"I liked it better when we went to Dr. Peter every week," he said to Sophie, instead of hello.

"We?" Mama said. She gave Sophie her gentle grin, which Sophie always figured was a lot like her own. Mama was small and elfish like her too, and her hair would be brown if she didn't streak it so it caught the light. "You never had a session with Dr. Peter, Zeke!"

"He's talking about the ice cream," Sophie said. "He knows you'll take him to Dairy Queen while you're waiting for me."

"Only now it's way too long between times," Zeke said. He puckered his forehead so that he looked like a miniature of Daddy. Except Daddy didn't wear his dark hair sticking up everywhere.

"Two weeks is not a long time," Mama said to him.

Sometimes it is, Sophie thought. Even back when they had first switched from twice a week to once a week, Sophie had felt like it was forever from one Dr. Peter visit to another. Now that she went only twice a month, she could store up so many things to talk to him about there was hardly time to spill it all out in the one hour they had.

But today I'm gonna talk about one thing, she told herself as Mama pulled up to the building, *and that's the showcase.*

As always, Dr. Peter was waiting for her at the front counter with his blue eyes twinkling behind his glasses and his mouth in a watermelon slice of a smile. Sophie loved those things about him—and the short, curly hair stiff with gel, and the faded freckles that danced on his face. She also liked it that he wasn't as tall as a lot of adults, especially Daddy, who towered over everybody. Daddy was getting better about not looking down at her, but Dr. Peter never had.

"Your shirt has four-leaf clovers on it!" Sophie said as she followed him back to the room where they always talked.

"St. Patrick's Day isn't far away," he said. "I'll be celebrating it all month."

"Why?" Sophie said. She settled herself on the window seat and selected one of the pillows shaped like a face. She always tried to pick one that had an expression to match what she was feeling. With the one wearing stern eyebrows and a straight yarn mouth firmly in her arms, she was ready.

"Because I'm Irish," Dr. Peter said. "And proud of it." He popped his eyes at Sophie. "Don't tell me you don't like corned beef and cabbage!"

"Yucko-poohy!" Sophie said. "No offense."

"None taken. Now …" He nodded at the pillow. "Do you want to tell me why you chose Mr. Determined to hold today?"

"Because I AM determined," Sophie said. "Do you want me to tell you why?"

Dr. Peter grinned. "Do I have a choice?"

Sophie plunged into the story, using different voices for the Flakes and the Pops and Miss Blythe, complete with her finger-making commas and question marks in the air. When she was finished she was out of breath. So was Dr. Peter.

"Whew!" he said. "That was some fast storytelling."

"I wanted plenty of time for us to discuss what I'm going to do," Sophie said.

Dr. Peter peered over the top of his glasses. Sophie did the same back with hers.

"What YOU are going to do?" he said. "Don't all the Corn Flakes have to decide?"

"We all have to agree," Sophie said. "But they expect me to come up with the best ideas because—well, that's the way it always is." She shrugged. "I'm not smarter—I've just had more practice thinking things up. And besides, I have to keep everybody from fighting. You know how they are."

Dr. Peter nodded soberly. Sophie had told him all about the problems the Corn Flakes had had in the past with Maggie being bossy and Kitty being afraid of her and Fiona being jealous of her because Sophie had gotten to like Maggie. It was Dr. Peter who had helped her figure out what the Corn Flakes Girls Guidelines should be. Things like no eye rolling.

"What's the worst that can happen if you don't come up with a brilliant idea for the group?" Dr. Peter said.

"Miss Blythe will give us some lame poem to recite and everybody will laugh at us and we'll get a bad grade and my father will take away my camera and there won't be any more Corn Flakes Productions and the Corn Pops will win and they will throw it smack-dab into our faces for the rest of our lives!"

Dr. Peter blinked at her behind his glasses. "All right then," he said. "I guess I'd better give you some help."

Sophie let out a relief sigh that came all the way from her heels, and she sank back into the pile of pillows. Dr. Peter pulled out his Bible, the one in the case with the frog on it. That was where the answers always were.

"How about a Jesus story?" he said.

"How about yes!"

"Now tell me again why we do this."

Sophie sat up straighter. "I can get to know Jesus better if I imagine him better, so then I'll know what to ask him and I'll know if the answer I think I'm getting later is really from him."

"You're amazing," Dr. Peter said. "I'm going to write down where the story is in the gospel for you to read later, because I want us to have time to talk about something else."

Sophie settled herself more comfortably while Dr. Peter wrote on a sticky note shaped like a shamrock.

"There you go. It's going to be a piece of corned beef for you to figure this one out."

"Don't you mean a piece of cake?" Sophie said.

"Nae, wee lass!" he cried in an accent Sophie had once heard from a policeman on an old Bugs Bunny cartoon. "It's corned beef I mean and so it is! In any case—you'll figure it out in the wink of an eye."

"And I'll report back to you in two weeks." Sophie tried to say it with the accent, but it came out sounding more like Bugs Bunny himself than the policeman.

"Ah—that's what I need to talk about." Dr. Peter rubbed his hand across his lips like he was erasing his Irish accent. When he spoke again it was in his real voice, the soft version. "You are doing so well, my friend," he said. "I wonder if you might like to try seeing me just once a month now."

No! Sophie wanted to shout. *No—I need you! How will I ever—*

"You've learned so much," Dr. Peter went on, "and you've come in week after week telling me all the ways you're using everything you've learned. Pretty soon you're going to be taking on clients of your own."

"But I still need you!" Sophie said. "Don't I?"

"Do you?" Dr. Peter said. "Think about it."

"I guess I know how to do my best in school now," she said slowly. "And I get along with my dad."

"Those are big. And do you need me to help you keep doing those things? Aren't you doing them on your own now?"

Sophie pulled a strand of hair under her nose, like a mustache. "I am," she said finally.

"Then be proud of yourself! I even have a reward for you."

Dr. Peter reached into a basket on the floor and pulled out two huge green top hats, which he popped onto their heads. Sophie's hung down over her eyes.

"Ah, you have a bit of the Irish now, you do!" he said.

Sophie let a silvery giggle escape from her throat, but then she wilted again.

"Talk to me," Dr. Peter said. His face beneath the hat's brim was serious and kind.

"I'm afraid," Sophie said. "What if I start messing up again?"

"I'll be right here if you need me."

"But how will I know if I really need you?"

"You mean, what would be the signs?"

She pumped her head up and down.

"Okay—one ..." He pulled up a stuffed finger on a pillow. "If you find yourself escaping into one of your characters when you shouldn't be—like in school or when your dad is talking to you—and you're doing it to hide from something painful, that would be a sign."

"Then I could ask Mama to call you for a session?"

"If—and this is number two." Dr. Peter lifted another puffy finger. "If your parents can't help you with whatever is bothering you that makes you want to escape into Antoinette or someone."

Sophie could feel her eyebrows pulling together.

"You can trust them, Sophie-Lophie-Loodle," he said.

At the sound of his nickname for her, Sophie thought she was going to cry. That was okay in Dr. Peter's office, but she still blinked back the tears.

"They've learned a lot from their sessions with me too," Dr. Peter said. "And they've already proved that they understand you better."

"I know," Sophie said. "But I'll miss you."

The tears did come then, and she let them stream down her face. Dr. Peter had always told her tears would help her wash away things that hurt.

"I'll miss you too, Loodle," he said. "But I'm still going to see you every month for as long as you need me."

"Promise?" she said.

Dr. Peter's face got soft and mushy. "I promise. I'll try not to let you down."

And because he said that, Sophie was able to feel a little bit proud. She decided that was going to be her high at the dinner table that night.

Every evening at supper lately, Daddy asked everyone to tell their high for the day and their low—the best thing that happened and the worst. Sophie was pretty sure he had learned that from Dr. Peter.

"My high is that I get to go on my first youth group retreat this weekend," Lacie burst out that night almost before they had said "Amen" to the blessing. "And my low is that I don't have anything to wear. Mama, could we please go to the mall?"

Lacie didn't look at Mama when she said it, but at Daddy.

Here we go, Sophie thought. *Lacie thinks she can get Daddy to do anything she wants him to.*

Of course, it seemed to her that it kind of made sense, since Lacie was so much like Daddy. She had his dark hair and his height—she was tall for a thirteen-year-old girl. And she played every sport in the world, just like he always had, and she made straight As—which Daddy still would if they gave grades at NASA, the space center where he was a scientist. Besides that, Lacie and Daddy were both organized and practical and didn't understand that much about being creative, not as far as Sophie could tell. What was creative about shooting a basketball into a hoop until even your hair was sweating?

"How much is this going to cost me?" Daddy said to Lacie.

"Nothing," Mama said. "She has more clothes than Dillard's as it is."

"Dillard's has an apostrophe," Zeke said.

While Mama and Daddy and Lacie all went nuts over how intelligent Zeke was, Sophie got herself geared up to deliver her high and low. She had an idea that just might work.

But Zeke got to go next because he was suddenly the child genius.

"High," he said. "I got banilla ice cream dipped in choc-lit at Dairy Queen."

Lacie gave a snort. "You can say 'apostrophe' but you can't pronounce 'vanilla'?"

"What was your low, Z?" Mama said.

Zeke frowned, his dark little eyebrows trying to hood his eyes. "I gotta wait a whole month before I get another one, because Sophie isn't going back to Dr. Peter 'til then."

"He just took my high!" Sophie said.

"But congratulations, Soph!" Daddy said. He gave a grin that was as big and square as his shoulders. "Go, girl."

"We're proud of you," Mama said.

Lacie surveyed Sophie as she swirled her fork through her veggie stir-fry. "Then how come you're still weird?" she said.

Daddy made a loud buzzing sound, which meant Lacie was not playing by team rules.

"I also had a low," Sophie said.

"Is it the same as your high?" Lacie said. "You totally have a crush on the guy."

No, Sophie wanted to say. *You are my low.* But instead she told them about the showcase and how Miss Blythe wouldn't let the Corn Flakes make a film.

"Bummer," Daddy said.

"It's a total suppression of our creative gifts!" Sophie said, Fiona-like.

Lacie looked at Daddy. "What did she just say?"

"So, Daddy," Sophie said, "could you and Mama please talk to Miss Blythe and tell her that we're really good at making films and they aren't lame—"

Lacie grunted.

"—and it's what we're going to do our whole lives so we should be allowed to—"

She stopped, because Daddy was pointing his fork at her. "Nice try, Soph," he said. "But it sounds like Miss Blythe knows what she's doing. I'm sure you and your crowd can come up with something else."

"I told you that you would be more well-rounded," Lacie said to her, "if you didn't spend all your time pretending you're Hannah Montana or somebody."

"Lacie," Mama said, "did you miss the part where Sophie already has a mother?"

Any other time, Sophie would have taken a minute to enjoy the fact that for once Lacie was the one getting in trouble. But right now she was staring at Daddy, watching her great idea dissolve in the discussion-over look on his face.

"Do you want to brainstorm together?" Mama said to Sophie.

Sophie shook her head.

She was missing Dr. Peter already.

Three

When Sophie got to school the next morning, she headed for the cafeteria. That was where the Corn Flakes met before classes when it was bad weather or they had something very private to discuss. It was their secret planning place—on the stage behind the closed curtains, way back in the corner where scenery from past performances lurked in the darkness.

As Sophie slipped behind the curtain, which was more dust than velvet, she spotted the shadowy Corn Flakes hunched together on hay bales left over from the second grade's Barnyard Showcase. She felt like she was wearing cement shoes as she trudged toward them, because she didn't have a scathingly brilliant idea. She didn't even have a lame one.

Maggie already had the Corn Flakes' Treasure Book out, as well as the peach gel pen. She definitely hadn't used up all its ink at their last meeting.

"Here's what I'm thinking," Fiona said before Sophie could even find a spot to sit on a bale of hay. "We should have our own auditions. We can each present our idea like we're performing it. That way we really see what it could look like."

Maggie wrote that down in neat, steady cursive, while Kitty's voice spiraled up into a whine Sophie was sure only dogs could hear.

"I don't know how to do that!" she said. "You're making it hard, Fiona."

Sophie could tell Fiona wanted to roll her eyes, but it was a Corn Flake rule that they weren't allowed to make each other—or anybody else—feel like they were dumb.

Kitty gave a nervous giggle. "Okay—well—mine's a thing my sisters and I used to do—"

"Show us," Fiona said.

"Okay—one of us sits on a chair like we're getting our hair fixed so whoever it is has a sheet on—only your hands are tied behind your back ...." She demonstrated. "And then somebody else gets behind that person, but under the sheet with only their arms sticking out—"

She fumbled with her arms for a minute and then directed Fiona to get behind her.

"So Fiona's the arms and you're everything else," Sophie said.

"Right, and then one of us that's left tells the girl in front to do different stuff like put on lipstick or comb her hair." Kitty's words were now coming out in giggle-bubbles. "Only it's the one behind with arms that does it, so—"

"Tell us to do something," Fiona said.

"Get down so you can't see what you're doing," Kitty said. "That's the best part."

Kitty was giggling so hard, Sophie had to laugh herself. "Brush your teeth," Sophie said.

"She doesn't have a toothbrush," Maggie said.

"Pretend."

Fiona grabbed an imaginary toothbrush and went after Kitty's teeth, landing halfway up her nostrils. Kitty let out a shriek.

"Pick your nose," Maggie said.

"No!" Kitty cried—but she leaned her face forward to poke out the little china-nose, and Fiona stuck a finger right into Kitty's ear.

Even Maggie was laughing now—a chuckle that came from somewhere down deep. "Feed yourself a banana," she said.

"Wash your hands first!" Sophie said.

"Why?" said Fiona.

"Because you just picked your nose!"

Suddenly a shaft of light shot straight back to them from the front of the stage, and an all-too-familiar voice said, "Oh, sick!"

The light got wider as the curtains opened and B.J. came toward them, followed by Anne-Stuart, who was already sneezing from the curtain dust.

"You're picking your nose, Kitty?" Anne-Stuart said.

"No," Fiona said. "I'm picking it for her."

Somebody else shrieked. Sophie recognized that as Willoughby, who was obviously hauling the curtains open in the wing.

"I should have known," said Queen Julia as she sailed through the opening. She stopped in front of Kitty and Fiona, who were now in the act of eating an invisible banana that was going everywhere but into Kitty's wide-open mouth.

"Tell me this isn't your showcase presentation," she said.

B.J. shook her butter-blonde bob. "If it is, don't count on a prize."

"Did you ask if you could use the stage to practice?" Anne-Stuart said. She gave a juicy sniff. "We have permission to practice our dance—"

"Every day before school," B.J. put in.

"Oh, yes?" Fiona said. "Well, we—"

"We're just leaving!" Sophie grabbed her backpack and stared hard at the other Corn Flakes.

Fiona's eyes turned into dashes, but she said, "Right — only because we're fair — which is more than I can say for —"

"Let's get our stuff!" Sophie said.

Kitty giggled. "Get ours, Fiona."

Fiona's arms flailed around Kitty until Maggie put a backpack in each of her hands and Fiona and Kitty shuffled out still attached. Sophie was sure Kitty was going to need CPR, she was giggling so hard.

Whew, that was close, Sophie thought as she followed Fiona and Kitty to the steps. If Fiona had kept at it, it would've gotten way ugly.

That was another Corn Flake rule — no being evil to the Corn Pops, no matter how nasty they were being.

"Hey, Maggie," Julia called across the stage.

Maggie turned slowly around, peach gel pen behind her ear. "Me?" she said.

Sophie watched Julia select the I-want-something-from-you smile and paste it on.

"Did you think about what I asked you yesterday?" she said.

"Yeah," Maggie said. Her voice was heavy.

"So — are you going to make our costumes?"

"We really want you to, Miss Maggie," Anne-Stuart said. She was smiling too and nodding her head like that would automatically get Maggie to nod hers.

B.J. bobbed her bob. "You'll get a good grade if you work with us."

"Maggie's with us," Fiona said.

"We stick together," Kitty said. "We're the Cor —"

"Let's get to class!" Sophie heard her voice squeak, which it usually did when she was trying to save her friends from disaster. If the Pops ever knew they called themselves the Corn Flakes, they would practically have to move out of town.

"Can you believe they even had the nerve to ask Maggie that?" Fiona said to the Flakes as they hurried down the hall to language arts class.

Kitty looped her arm through Maggie's. "I would never let them take you away from us," she said.

Sophie was just forming a picture in her mind of Kitty hurling herself in front of Maggie like she was shielding her from an oncoming train, when Maggie said, "We're not really going to do that arm thing for our performance, are we?"

They all stopped in front of the classroom door and Kitty, Maggie, and Fiona looked at Sophie.

"Well," Sophie said carefully. "It was a good idea—but it wasn't a brilliant one. I know the Corn Flakes are capable of doing something really fabulous!"

She didn't have a chance to see how Kitty and Fiona were taking that because Mr. Denton called to them as he came toward them down the hall, leading a tall girl with reddish hair cut short and splashy.

"This is Darbie," Mr. Denton said. "She's joining our class."

The girl, who Sophie now saw from close up had dark eyes and smooth milky-white skin, didn't look to Sophie like she was "joining" anything. The way she seemed to be smelling at the air, it was more like she was starting her first day in a garbage dump.

I know how you feel, Sophie thought. *I despised being the new girl too. Hardly anybody even knew I was here until Fiona came.*

"Hi," Fiona said. "Where'd you move from?"

"Northern Ireland," Darbie said.

Sophie felt her eyes widen. "Ireland!"

"The real Ireland?" Kitty said.

29

"No, silly, the fake one," Fiona said. She smiled at Darbie again. "She doesn't get out that much."

"What's it like there?" Maggie said.

"Are there really leprechauns?" Kitty said.

Darbie didn't answer.

"Ladies—you sound like a bevy of reporters." Mr. Denton gave them his dial-tone-dry look. "Let's get Darbie settled in before we start interrogating her."

"I'm Kitty!" Kitty said as Mr. Denton led Darbie into the classroom.

"I'm Fiona—she's Maggie," Fiona said.

Even after they got into the classroom, Sophie didn't introduce herself because Darbie didn't appear to be listening, not the way she took herself to the other side of the room and stood with her back to them, straight and stiff-looking. Besides, an image was forming in Sophie's mind—of being from a foreign country and coming to an American school—*so proud of her homeland and yet so eager to belong. She was wearing a dress with green shamrocks on it, and a green derby—and carried a lunch box full of corned beef and cabbage—*

Okay, so she'd have to get Fiona to do some research on Ireland.

She tossed her hair in an Irish way—whatever that was—

"Hey, you—Soapy."

Sophie blinked into the face of Julia.

Just when she was getting to the good part. "What?" Sophie said.

"Who's the new girl?" Julia was wearing her we-really-are-friends-sometimes expression.

"Her name's Darbie," Sophie said. "She's from Ireland."

Julia looked almost impressed. "She dresses cute for being from a foreign country," she said. "Sometimes they dress funny."

"Those are all new clothes," Anne-Stuart said, sniffing as though she could smell their just-bought-ness.

"Old Navy," B.J. said.

Sophie edged away from the Corn Pops. It felt germy to be so close to them while they were sizing up Darbie from across the room.

"Go ask her if she wants to sit with us," Julia said to Willoughby.

Willoughby nodded her head of pecan-colored wavy hair and headed for the back of the room where Fiona was showing Darbie how to unlock her locker.

"I think she's sitting with us," Sophie said.

"She doesn't look weird at all," B.J. said. "She's more like us."

"Tell that Harley girl to move so Darbie can sit next to me," Julia said to B.J.

Sophie moved away, sure she had Corn-Pop-itis crawling all over her.

The Corn Flakes watched, mouths open, as Willoughby ushered Darbie to the seat B.J. had cleared for her, and Julia scooted her desk close to Darbie's, and Anne-Stuart provided her with gel pens, paper, and a container of lip gloss.

By lunch, Darbie was sitting at the Pops' table with a buffet in front of her that Julia had sent Willoughby through the line for with a wad of dollar bills.

At after-lunch free time, Julia and Anne-Stuart hustled Darbie off to a corner of the school yard, each with an arm around her. B.J. was walking backward in front of them and Willoughby trailed along behind, shrieking for no reason that Sophie could figure out.

"I guess she's going to be a Corn Pop," Kitty said as the Flakes lined up against the fence.

"Whether she wants to or not," Fiona said. "They haven't even given her a chance to talk to anybody else. That's so 'them.'"

"Hey," Maggie said, pointing a squared-off finger. "Look what they're doing."

Kitty squinted. "What ARE they doing?"

Sophie brushed away the hair the March wind tousled into her face. The Pops were now standing on the cement walk-way along the fence, all in a row with Darbie in the middle. Everyone was watching Julia, who was moving like she was putting on an invisible pair of pantyhose.

"I know," Fiona said. "They're teaching her their dance."

"She's auditioning!" Kitty said.

Sure enough, as Sophie and the Flakes watched, Darbie imitated Julia—looking more like she was putting on over-alls than nylons. The other Pops joined in, exaggerating their motions with Julia clapping her hands in rhythm and calling out, "One, two, three."

Suddenly, Darbie stopped and put up her hands.

"She hates it," Fiona whispered.

Julia and the other three stepped off the sidewalk and stood back. Darbie was still for a few seconds, and then she moved her feet, faster and faster, in little kicks and stomps while the rest of her body stayed straight and she kept her head faced forward.

"How cool is that?" Fiona said.

Maggie nodded. "I've seen that on TV."

"It must be Irish," Kitty said.

Sophie could almost feel her own Irish character—who so far had no name—holding her shamrock-dotted skirt up to her knees and moving her feet so fast the crowd could hardly see them. *When the music stopped, they all rushed to her—*

"You don't do it as good as Darbie does, Sophie," Maggie said.

"Come on," Fiona said as the bell rang. She linked her arm through Sophie's as they followed the crowd toward the door. "You were thinking Irish, weren't you?"

"We have to make an Irish film," Sophie said.

"Oh, definitely," Fiona said. "I'll find out stuff on the Internet."

Maggie looked over her shoulder at them as they shuffled their way into the hall. "We have to think of something for our showcase first."

"Shhh . . ." Kitty said. "Don't let the Pops hear we don't have our idea yet."

The Corn Pops were just ahead of them, but Sophie could see that they were way too focused on Darbie to give them a second thought.

"Can you teach us how to do that?" she heard Willoughby say to her.

"But we're not doing that for the showcase," Julia said — eyes flashing at Willoughby.

Anne-Stuart put her arm around Darbie's shoulder with a sniff. "We can teach you how to really dance. You're coordinated enough. It won't take that long."

Darbie stopped just inside the arts classroom and flung Anne-Stuart's arm away from her.

"I know how to 'really dance,' so I do," she said. "Would you ever lay off? Scram!"

Miss Blythe glided over to where the Flakes and Pops were now standing in two clumps with Darbie between them.

"Artistic differences?" Miss Blythe said. She made it sound like that was a good thing.

"Darbie's going to be in our group," Anne-Stuart said. "And we were just telling her—"

"—that I don't know how to dance."

"It's just not the right dance for us," Anne-Stuart said.

"—then cop on and find someone else," Darbie said.

The Corn Pops stared at her, probably because nobody ever said no to them. In the silence, Maggie spoke up.

"I'm doing costumes for you," she said to Julia.

Sophie could feel her eyes popping at Maggie. "You're doing costumes for them?"

"I don't WANT to," Maggie said, "but I HAVE to." She frowned. "It's my mom."

"Oh," Sophie said. She knew about parents and "have to's."

"My mom said if we didn't get an idea by today, I have to do costumes for the Po—for them."

"What?" Fiona said.

"That works out just perfectly then," Miss Blythe said. "Without Maggie, your group needs another person, Fiona. And since—what was your name, love?" She glanced at Darbie's NEW STUDENT slip.

Darbie's eyes turned to stones. "Darbie O'Grady," she said. "Not 'love.'"

Miss Blythe clasped her hands under her chin. Sophie wasn't sure what punctuation mark that was.

"Fabulous," Miss Blythe said. "Darbie O'Grady, you will work with Fiona and Kitty and Sophie. Maggie, you'll transfer to the Julia, B.J., Willoughby, and Anne-Stuart group."

When the Corn Flakes got to their table, Kitty was already whining like a cocker spaniel.

"Why did they have to steal Maggie? Who's going to make our costumes?"

"What costumes?" Fiona said. "We don't even have an idea yet."

34

"Now isn't that just brilliant." Darbie folded her arms across the front of her sweater. "I've gone from one set of eejits to another, so I have."

"I love how you talk," Kitty said to her. "Say something else."

Darbie didn't cooperate. She seemed to be chewing at the inside of her mouth.

"Do you miss being in Ireland?" Kitty said.

"That depends on whether she's from Ireland or Northern Ireland," Fiona said. She turned to Sophie. "They're two different countries."

"I told you Northern Ireland before," Darbie said, and then she clamped her teeth together.

"Oh—too bad," Fiona said.

"Why is it too bad?" Kitty said.

"It is not bad!" Darbie glared at each one of them in turn. "It's my home and I'll be thanking you not to be slagging it."

It wasn't hard to figure out what "slagging" meant. "We don't mean to," Sophie said. "We're just curious."

"Insatiably," Fiona said.

"It's because we love to make films about fascinating things," Sophie said. "Even though Miss Blythe won't let us do one for the showcase, we still want to make an Irish film for Corn Flakes Productions—that's what we're called."

"So you're only chatting me up so you can use me." Darbie's eyes were like flickers of heat lightning. "I wouldn't be part of one of your childish little pictures. You see ..." she lowered her voice so that the Corn Flakes had to tilt themselves toward her to hear. "I am not a child."

Four

It was a long-faced group that met at Fiona's house the next morning, Saturday, to try to make a decision about the showcase.

Fiona was annoyed because her little brother and sister, Rory and Isabella, were being even more heinous than usual, breaking in the new nanny, Ethel, who stood in the middle of the yard and yelled because she was the biggest human being in the world and couldn't run after them.

Kitty was all whimpery because Maggie wasn't there.

Sophie was still smoldering over the fact that the Corn Pops got to do what they were good at for the showcase, but the Corn Flakes couldn't.

And as for Darbie—it seemed to Sophie that she was sullen and annoyed and smoldering no matter what was going on.

It was a warm day for March. They were sprawled at the picnic table on Fiona's back deck with their juice boxes, sighing and staring, when Darbie gave her wristwatch a pointy look and said, "It's half eleven. We've sat here foostering about for an hour now."

Kitty giggled. "Half eleven? Does that mean eleven thirty?"

"It means we need to be getting on with it," Darbie said.

"You come up with something then," Fiona said.

Darbie shrugged. Fiona broke rule number one and rolled her eyes. Kitty giggled again, although as far as Sophie could see there was absolutely nothing funny. She could almost hear the poem Miss Blythe was going to assign them.

The door to the deck opened and Boppa, Fiona's grandfather, strolled toward them, a picnic basket in each hand. "How's the showcase coming along?" he said.

"It's not," Fiona said. "Let's face it—we're clueless."

"Sounds like you lasses need a break."

Boppa was wiggling his dark caterpillar eyebrows, but today not even Boppa and his comical faces could cheer up the Corn Flakes.

"Lasses?" Kitty said.

Boppa stopped next to Darbie and gave her his soft smile. "Do they still call young ladies 'lasses' in Ireland these days? It's been a while since I've been there. I don't want to be uncool."

"No," Darbie said between her teeth. "Not in NORTHERN Ireland."

"So you don't say 'wee' and 'bonnie' either?" Sophie said.

"Only American tourists who think they know everything talk that way in my country." Darbie's words came out tightly, as if she were constantly trying to swallow them back. "And I thought I told you I wasn't a specimen under a microscope."

"Doesn't anybody want to know where we're going to eat this lunch?" Boppa said.

"Uh, let me think," Fiona said. "Here at the table?"

"How does Gull Island sound?"

"Really?" Kitty said.

"That would be great, Boppa," Fiona said, "if we actually had a boat." She was just short of rolling her eyes. Fiona got a little cranky when she was frustrated.

"We do today. I rented a couple of rowboats so you could get out to the island for a picnic lunch."

Sophie jolted, knocking over her grape juice box. "A real boat? Does it have paddles?"

"It would be murder to row without them," Darbie said. She glared and set the box upright just before purple juice dripped out onto her sleeve.

But Sophie barely heard her. All through stuffing themselves into the black SUV—with Boppa, Ethel, Rory, and Izzy, and riding to Messick Point, Sophie could only think about Colleen O'Bravo, who was headed for adventure.

That's my Irish character's name, Sophie thought. *And Colleen isn't going to call people eejits, which I guess is a word for stupid people, but I'm sure not going to ask Darbie. Darbie's mean—Colleen isn't.*

While Boppa parked the car, Ethel led the group down a pier that stretched over the water, barking down at Izzy and Rory who she had clamped firmly by their forearms. She sounded like a jail warden, but Sophie tried to imagine her with an accent. *Maybe she was an Irish jail warden, and the Corn Flakes were trying to break Darbie out of prison, where she had been unjustly sent.* She wasn't sure how Rory and Izzy were going to fit in. Maybe they were rats ...

"I'll be in one boat with the two little ones," Ethel was shouting, "and Mr. Bunting will be in the other one with the rest of you." She sized Sophie up with her eyes. "You're little, so that boat can handle it."

"I'm not so sure the other one can handle HER," Fiona whispered to Sophie.

"Everybody put on a life jacket," Ethel shouted next.

Darbie opened her mouth just as Ethel shoved a blue puffy thing at her chest.

"I don't think you argue with her," Kitty whispered.

By the time Boppa joined them with the picnic baskets, the girls were all strapped into their jackets. Sophie's was so big even over her sweatshirt, she could barely see where she was going. Ethel was still trying to wrestle the two little ones into theirs.

"Any of you ever rowed a boat before?" Boppa said to the girls.

Darbie's hand shot up. Fiona raised hers too.

"When was that?" Boppa said to her.

"That one summer," Fiona said. "We went up to that lake place in Michigan. You weren't there."

"You get back here, Izzy, before you fall in and get soaked!"

Ethel thundered past them with Rory under one arm. Boppa pointed down to one of the boats.

"Get aboard," he said. "I'll be right back." Then he took off after Ethel, just in time to catch Rory kicking himself free.

"I'd throw both of those little blaggards into the drink," Darbie said as she led the way down the ladder.

"Don't you mean black guards?" Fiona said. "I think that's the way it's spelled."

Darbie shrugged. "Then maybe you shouldn't think."

Kitty gave one of her I'm-about-to-cry giggles. "Boppa said to get in the boat."

It took a few minutes to sort out the seating arrangements. Fiona said she should be in front so she could be captain, and Darbie should be at the other end to take orders. After Darbie was in her place at the back of the boat, she smirked and said Fiona could sit up in the bow if she wanted to, but if she expected to help row she had to sit there next to Darbie in the middle.

"I know," Fiona said. "I was just checking to be sure YOU knew."

"Right," Darbie said.

Sophie and Kitty sat in the stern—without oars—and Fiona told them to get on their knees and lean against the seat since that was the right way to do it.

"It would be if we were canoeing," Darbie said. "In this boat, you can sit on your bum."

"I have a 'bum'?" Kitty said.

"I think that's her word for bottom," Sophie said. She added that to her mental treasury of Colleen words.

Darbie nodded at the two oars which were attached to the boat through big metal clamps. Darbie called them *oarlocks*. "You're going to have to row precisely in time with me," she said to Fiona, "unless you fancy turning around in circles."

Sophie saw a smile escape from Darbie's dark eyes.

She's making fun of Fiona, Colleen O'Bravo thought. I will speak to her about that, I will, when we're alone. Then she settled on her bum and waited for the adventure to begin.

But that didn't promise to happen any time soon. Up on the dock, Ethel was holding Izzy between her knees as she tried to poke her arms through the life jacket holes. Boppa was working on Rory, and both kids were screaming, and Fiona's eyes were practically rolling right out of her head and into the water.

"She's got one done, so she does," Darbie said.

Boppa grabbed Izzy as she wriggled away from Ethel and held her by the back of the life jacket with one hand and Rory with the other. He was wrinkling his caterpillar eyebrows from Ethel to the boat and back again.

"He knows somebody's going to drown," Fiona said. "So much for this adventure."

"Could you drown here?" Kitty said. She pulled herself closer to Sophie. "How deep is it?"

"It's not but a meter or two deep right here," Darbie said.

"How do you know?" Fiona said.

"Because I live on the water. My kinfolk are fishermen," Darbie shot back.

"We don't talk in meters."

"Everybody else in the whole world does."

"Fiona."

Boppa was squatting on the dock, looking down at them.

"Ethel is going to stay here with Izzy, and I'm going to take Rory in the other boat. Can you follow me, do you think?"

"Absolutely," Fiona said. She grabbed up the oar. "Untie us, Sophie!"

"Cast off," Darbie said.

"WhatEVER," Fiona said back.

"I don't think they like each other that much," Kitty whispered to Sophie.

Sophie tried to imagine she was Colleen, unwrapping the rope from the barnacled deck and pushing against the piling with her hand to send them off, but it was impossible. Darbie and Fiona were definitely not in a dream world.

"You sure you know what you're doing?" Darbie said to Fiona.

"I told you, I've done it before," Fiona said.

Sophie watched Darbie push her oar backward over the water, dip it in, and pull it back.

"In time with me!" Darbie said.

"Why do you get to be the captain?" Fiona said.

"Go on, then."

Darbie pulled her oar out of the water. Fiona pushed hers down into the water and then lifted it up. The boat went backward.

"That's not the way Darbie did it," Kitty whispered to Sophie.

It didn't take a sailor to figure out Darbie's was the right way. The boat was now moving in a circle.

"You're making a bags of doing it!" Darbie called out. "Do it like this! Forward. Now in! Now back!"

"You got us going in circles!" Fiona shouted back.

"No—YOU do! Now quit blathering and do what I tell you!"

Fiona dragged her oar in the water, and the boat came to a stop. Kitty edged closer to Sophie.

"You all right back there?" Boppa was holding Rory between his feet and watching the girls.

"We're fine!" Fiona said.

Darbie gave a knot of a laugh. "We would be if you would admit you don't know what you're doing and listen to me!"

"Shut up!" Fiona said. "I know what I'm doing. This is an American boat—not Irish!"

"You're an eejit!"

Kitty clutched at Sophie's jeans and started to cry. At that point, Sophie had no choice. She had to escape into Colleen O'Bravo's world or she was going to push Darbie and Fiona and Kitty right into the shallows of the Chesapeake.

Why are they arguing about silly things when there's work to be done? Colleen thought. She didn't know exactly what work it was, what incredibly important mission she'd be assigned, but she certainly wasn't going to find out this way. Even though that angry Darbie O'Grady finally got the boat to move through the water in a straight line, her fellow crew members refused to concentrate on what their mission might be. Those two with the oars are too busy trying to both be captain, she thought with a little anger of her own. And I suppose it's up to me as always, to step in and settle things between them so we can get on with it. She gathered her shamrock-dotted skirts up around her knees and stood up, one foot on the bench where her bum had just been. "Now see here ..." she began. But they all screamed at her at once, even Kitty. In fact, she screamed loudest, as the boat lurched and—

—and Sophie tumbled backward into the water with Kitty still attached to her pant leg. All she could hear was Darbie yelling, "Are you gone in the head? Sit DOWN!"

Five

Sunday was a bumpy day, and it got rougher with each piece of news Sophie stumbled over.

Right after church, Kitty called, still wailing. As far as Sophie could tell, she hadn't stopped bawling since before the boat had even dumped them out.

"No offense, Kitty," Sophie said, "but are you still crying? You hardly even went under the water. You were wearing a life jacket!"

"That's not what's wrong!" Kitty said. She sounded like a cat being bathed in the sink.

Sophie sighed. "Then what is wrong?"

"My dad said I can't go over to Fiona's anymore!"

"*What?* Why?"

"Because her parents didn't watch us."

"Her parents never watch us. They're not even there most of the time."

"Yeah. That's what my dad said. He said I could've drowned, and he's not taking any more chances."

Sophie nibbled at her lip. This wasn't the time to point out that if Kitty hadn't carried on so much when her dad had arrived to pick her up, he probably wouldn't have thought she'd been near death.

"Are you guys going to stop being my friend because I can't go to Fiona's?" Kitty said, winding up again.

"Hello! You're a Corn Flake!" Sophie said.

That seemed to calm Kitty down for the time being.

The next phone call was from Fiona. She wasn't crying, as far as Sophie could tell.

"My mom and dad fired Ethel," she said, voice cheery. "It's because she can't control the brats." Fiona gave a soft snort. "I could've told them that."

"That means another new nanny," Sophie said. "I wish Kateesha hadn't quit. I liked her."

"So did her fiancé. They went off and got married, which I think is dumb. Anyway, here's the bad news: Boppa has to watch the two little morons until my parents get around to hiring somebody, so no more Boppa adventures for us for a while. We can't even meet out at my house."

Sophie sagged against the step she was sitting on with the phone. "It's all my fault."

"They didn't terminate her because of the boat thing," Fiona said. "That stuff happens, they said. Besides, you're not to blame—Darbie is. She just thinks she's the boss of us, that's all, and she didn't even know what she was doing."

"I'm the one who freaked out and stood up!" Sophie said. *Gone in the head*, was the way Darbie had said it.

Fiona's voice went down to secret level. "And I know why too. You were coming up with a new character—somebody Irish, right? What's her name?"

Before Sophie could answer, she heard what sounded like the Tasmanian Devil on Fiona's end of the line.

"I have to go help Boppa shut them up," Fiona said. "Mom was up all night doing surgery on somebody's stomach. She is not going to be happy if they wake her up."

Sophie turned off the phone and curled up miserably on the step. All she wanted to do was slip into Colleen's world, where she wasn't responsible for nannies getting fired and people's dads saying they couldn't go to other people's houses. But as deliciously as Colleen beckoned to her with her red ringlets dancing—she had to have her hair in red ringlets—Sophie felt an old uneasy squirminess in her stomach. Colleen might be brave and determined and ready to take any risk for the cause—whatever that might be—but she could also get Sophie into a lot of trouble, and Sophie knew it. First would be the escapes into Colleen's world—then the bad grades—then the loss of the camera.

And she and the Corn Flakes would still end up reciting "Mary Had a Little Lamb" for the stupid showcase.

There's only one person who can help me now, she decided as she uncurled herself from the step. *I need to tell Mama and Daddy it's time for me to go back to Dr. Peter.*

The only two good things about the day so far were that Lacie was still away on her youth group retreat and Zeke was taking a nap. Those were God signs, as far as Sophie was concerned. She never, ever had Mama and Daddy all to herself.

She found them both in the family room, faces in the Sunday paper. When Sophie slipped onto the couch beside Mama, she folded the paper in her lap. Daddy woke up behind his.

"I need to talk to you," Sophie said. "Dr. Peter said I could come see him any time I started back into my old habits, and I've started."

She drew in a huge breath. Daddy tossed the paper to the floor and leaned forward in the big chair with his hands folded between his blue-jeaned knees.

"Good job, coming to us before it got out of hand, Soph," he said. "That's heads-up ball." Daddy always talked like the whole family was playing in the Super Bowl.

46

"Then Mama can make me an appointment?" Sophie said. "For tomorrow?"

Her parents did that thing they always did — looking at each other over the top of her head like they were having an entire conversation without saying a word. Kind of the way she and Fiona did sometimes.

"You know, Dream Girl," Mama said, "Daddy and I have been seeing Dr. Peter too, and we can probably help you with this."

Sophie nodded slowly. Dr. Peter had mentioned that, come to think of it. Still — she pulled a strand of hair under her nose.

"What?" Daddy said. "Come on, give us the goods."

"I don't know if you can do it like Dr. Peter," Sophie said.

Daddy grinned at Mama. "You have to admit, she's honest."

"You haven't seen us in action," Mama said. "We've been waiting for an opportunity like this."

"We've been in training." Daddy flexed his arm muscles, and a giggle slipped out of Sophie.

"What?" Daddy said. "What's funny?"

"So — you'll really, like, help me and not just take the camera away if my grades drop?"

"Absolutely," Mama said.

"All right, let's go — bring it on," Daddy said.

Mama got out some lemon bars and milk, and Sophie launched into the story. By the time she got to the part about Fiona's parents firing Ethel, she was feeling like she *was* talking to Dr. Peter. Mama and Daddy were listening and nodding, and they didn't interrupt once.

And then the front door burst open, slapping against the wall — and Lacie appeared.

She wasn't alone. There was a lady behind her with a face so twisted in anger, it took Sophie a minute to realize it was Lacie's best friend Valerie's mom. An *uh-oh* took shape in

Sophie's mind. Mrs. Bonningham had been a chaperone on the youth group retreat.

Mama and Daddy must have seen the smoke coming out of the lady's ears too, because they skipped the whole how-was-the-trip-what-are-you-doing-home-so-early thing and went straight to "What's wrong?"

Lacie opened her mouth, but it was Mrs. Bonningham who spewed out several paragraphs worth of stuff about Lacie being caught outside her cabin, after curfew, with a BOY.

"We weren't doing anything!" Lacie managed to get in. "We were just talking!" Even her freckles were pale.

"What were you thinking?" Daddy said. His face was watermelon red.

"Whatever it was, they were all thinking the same thing," Mrs. Bonningham said. "Half the kids were off someplace, and most of them weren't 'just talking.'"

Sophie didn't even want to *think* about what that meant.

Mrs. Bonningham pulled her neck up in a stiff way. "Let's just say the whole thing was less than spiritually focused. I don't think I heard God mentioned a single time except when they were blessing the food."

"It was just supposed to be fun!" Lacie wailed.

"Well, the fun's about to be over," Daddy said.

He ushered Lacie up the stairs, and Mama steered Mrs. Bonningham toward the front door. When Mama too had hurried up the steps to Lacie's room, Sophie was left on the couch with a half-empty plate of lemon bars. They were the last thing she wanted.

Here we go again, she thought as she trudged up to her own room. *Lacie has a crisis and instantly it's all about her. Forget about the devastation that's happening in MY life!*

Although she was way tempted to jump with both feet into Colleen's world and forget about her own currently miserable one, Sophie flopped down on her bed and tried to think what Dr. Peter would tell her to do.

Du-uh, she thought, hitting herself on the forehead with the heel of her hand. *He'd say, "Have you read that Bible story, Loodle?"*

She pulled out her Bible and turned each thin page between the tips of her fingers. She always did that. It seemed more sacred that way.

"Okay, John thirteen," she said out loud — mostly to drown out the deep thunder of Daddy's voice rolling out of Lacie's room next door. She didn't see how Zeke was sleeping through all this.

The pages splashed softly to chapter 13, verse 1, and Sophie read.

It was just before the Passover Feast. Jesus knew that the time had come for him to leave this world and go to the Father. Having loved his own who were in the world, he now showed them the full extent of his love.

Sophie stopped and closed her eyes. Dr. Peter had taught her to pretend she was somebody in the story, which was challenging this time, seeing how all the disciples were boys. Trying not to think about the Fruit Loops, Sophie changed her name to Luke and pulled her hair under her nose like a mustache. It wasn't her favorite role, but at least she got to be with Jesus. She read on.

The evening meal was being served . . . Jesus got up from the meal, took off his outer clothing —

Yikes! Sophie thought. *Okay, that has to be just like a jacket or something.*

Sophie got a firmer grip on the sides of the Bible and focused hard on being Luke.

Sophie/Luke read on, scratching at his mustache.

Jesus wrapped a towel around his waist. After that, he poured water into a basin and began to wash his disciples' feet, drying them with the towel that was wrapped around him.

Sophie/Luke yanked his feet back as Jesus worked his way down the table toward him. *My feet are way dirty!* he thought. *I've been running around in sandals all day! This is SO embarrassing!*

And then suddenly, Jesus was right there next to him, reaching out for Simon Peter's ankle. Simon Peter said to him,

"Lord, are you going to wash my feet?"

That's what I wanna know! Sophie/Luke thought. He pulled the edges of his dirty robe over the tips of his toes.

Jesus replied, "You do not realize now what I am doing, but later you will understand."

I sure hope so, thought Sophie/Luke. Right now his mind felt like a bowl of pudding.

"No," said Peter, "you shall never wash my feet."

Tell him, Peter! Sophie/Luke wanted to cry out. Tell him we're not worthy to have our Master touch our filthy feet! After all, if anyone could change Jesus' mind, it was Peter. He was the biggest and the strongest.

Jesus answered, "Unless I wash you, you have no part with me."

"Then, Lord," Simon Peter replied, "Not just my feet but my hands and my head as well!"

Let me just jump right into the bowl! Sophie/Luke thought. *That's how much help I need right now!*

Sophie stopped and scanned down the page with her finger. When was she going to get to the part where the answer to the showcase problem was?

She stopped at verse 12. *When he had finished washing their feet he put on his clothes and returned to his place.* Sophie/Luke watched his every move. The answer was sure to come right from the Master's lips.

"Now that I, your Lord and Teacher, have washed your feet, you also should wash one another's feet. I have set you an example that you should do as I have done for you."

Sophie blinked and let her "mustache" drop to her shoulder. That was all Dr. Peter had said to read. But what did any of that have to do with the major catastrophe she was in the middle of?

She tried to picture herself taking a bowl and pitcher to school tomorrow and breaking it out in arts class and washing Kitty's and Fiona's and Darbie's feet. Miss Blythe might think it was artistic genius, but the Corn Pops—not to mention Darbie—would roll their eyes right up into their brains.

I would so do it, Jesus, Sophie thought. *I totally would. Only, I just don't get how it's going to help us come up with an idea and keep me out of trouble.*

There was a shriek from next door, which popped the image of Jesus out of Sophie's head like a pin in a bubble. It was Lacie, begging for mercy.

"PLEASE don't make me drop softball!" she was practically screaming. "I have to play—I have to—Coach was gonna pick me as team captain."

Mama's voice murmured something and Daddy's muttered something back and Lacie went into a new burst of hysterical tears. Sophie figured there must be a flood in that room by now.

This could go on forever, Sophie thought as she threw herself back against her pillows. *So much for Mama and Daddy helping me with my problem.*

She closed her eyes and let Colleen in, tossing her red ringlets and assuring Sophie that everything would turn out, it just would.

But as Sophie donned her green top hat, she thought again of Dr. Peter.

She needed him, and she needed him now.

Six

The next three days were so foot-stomping frustrating, Sophie wanted to pitch a fit about every other minute. But Lacie was doing enough of that for both of them.

Whenever Mama and Daddy weren't both dealing *with* Lacie, they were talking to each other *about* Lacie. Or they were on the phone discussing with other people the whole church youth group "situation."

What about MY situation? Sophie wanted to scream more than once.

One of those times was Monday, when right in front of everybody before school on the playground, the Pops acted out the whole arm scene they had witnessed the Flakes doing on the stage that one morning. They didn't use names, but everybody knew, because there wasn't a kid gathered there who didn't turn and gape at the Corn Flakes or laugh so hard they were spewing spit, like the Fruit Loops did.

"Those boys could be a little more obnoxious," Fiona muttered to Sophie, "but I don't know how."

And then, during arts class, while the Corn Flakes continued to scribble down ideas and crumple them up and feel lamer by the minute, the Pops got to go to the stage and practice their dance.

"Like they really need to practice," Maggie told the Corn Flakes after class. "I watched them rehearse all weekend — and you want to know what?"

"No," Fiona said. "But tell us anyway."

Maggie pulled her head forward, and so did Sophie, Kitty, and Fiona. "Their parents are spending so much money on fabric for the costumes," she whispered. "I'm not supposed to tell you what they're going to look like, but they're expensive."

Right on cue, Kitty whimpered.

By Tuesday, the Corn Flake group still hadn't come up with an idea, and Darbie had grown more and more "disdainful," as Fiona put it.

"Does that mean she thinks we're absurd and stupid and lame?" Sophie said before school.

"Pretty much."

"I don't like her," Kitty whispered — even though they were huddled in a far corner of the school yard and Darbie wasn't even outside. "I don't like her at all."

"Yeah, but we're stuck with her," Fiona said. She wiggled her eyebrows. "As soon as the showcase is over though, whammo — she's out of here. We don't ever even have to talk to her again."

Sophie toyed with the string on her hooded sweatshirt.

"What, Soph?" Fiona said. "Don't tell me you want to be friends with her! She acts like we have head lice or something. She's as bad as the Corn Pops."

"Only she treats them the same way she does us," Sophie said.

"I even saw her blow Harley and them off," Kitty said. "She just doesn't like anybody."

"I don't get it," Sophie said.

Fiona pulled a splinter of wood off the fence and poked it at the ground. "We don't have to 'get it.' If she doesn't want to be friends with anybody, then what are we supposed to do?"

Wash her feet, Sophie thought.

She put her hand over her mouth, just in case she had said it out loud, but neither Kitty nor Fiona was looking at her like she suddenly had three nostrils, so she figured she was safe. That thought had been pretty crazy, even for her.

But it wouldn't leave her alone all day Tuesday: *Everybody needs at least one friend.* When she herself had moved to Poquoson from Houston, all she'd wanted was one girlfriend who would understand her and not think she was whacked out—and she had prayed for that even before Dr. Peter had taught her about talking to Jesus. Then, just like in one of her own daydreams, Fiona had suddenly been there.

Sophie wasn't sure what to do with that. But during social studies, when Ms. Quelling assigned a country project, she decided it couldn't hurt to pick Ireland. She was the first one in line for the library.

She found one book that had information about Northern Ireland too, and she burrowed into it before the bell rang. She found out that Irish people dug up some kind of dirt called peat to use for firewood, and that the whole country had almost died out when there had been a potato famine back in 1845. That tickled up a scene for the film, but it didn't help much when she got to arts class and Darbie demanded to know just HOW they were going to make a holy show of themselves in the showcase.

"I know we will," she said, arms folded across her sweater. "It's only a matter of how we're to be mortified."

Sophie didn't want to wash Darbie's feet at that point. It was one of those moments when she had the urge to clench her fists and stomp her foot and scream, "Then why don't you think of something if you're so smart!"

She didn't have to. Fiona did it. Darbie told her she didn't need to eat the head off her. Then Kitty started crying. And Miss Blythe floated over to them and assured them that the best art was born out of frustration.

Miss Blythe walked toward the Fruit Loops, calling, "Art is discipline, boys!"

Darbie scowled. "I don't want to give birth to art, thank you very much."

She said "much" like "mooch." Sophie made a note to talk like that when she was being Colleen O'Bravo. At the moment, Colleen had "mooch" to be concerned about.

Would there be enough peat for the winter? Would there be a peat shortage, just as there had been a five-year potato famine those many years ago that had almost brought Ireland to ruin? Some of her own ancestors had come to America because of that — and now she was here too — and no one seemed to understand her a bit —

"You — Sophie!"

Sophie tossed Colleen's red ringlets out of her face and stared blankly at Darbie.

"I thought you'd gone into a bit of a trance," Darbie said. "I hope you were coming up with something."

"She will," Kitty said. "She always does."

All Darbie did was grunt.

At home that night, it was impossible for Sophie to think about the showcase, much less come up with something. Lacie and Mama and Daddy were having yet another "discussion" in Lacie's room, and Sophie had to watch Zeke in her room and try to do her homework at the same time. At least she got to read about Northern Ireland, although Zeke made even that pretty hard when he tried to climb up Sophie's curtains like Spider-Man. Finally, she made him sit next to her on the floor and listen while she read the book out loud.

"'The splitting of Ireland into the Republic of Ireland and Northern Ireland took place in 1921,'" she read.

"Was I born yet?" Zeke said.

"No. Mama and Daddy weren't even born yet. I don't know anybody that was born then." Sophie patted the top of Zeke's head. "You have to listen. We're about to get to the good part."

"Is Spider-Man in it?"

"No!"

Zeke's dark eyebrows came down into upside-down Vs. "Then how's it going to get good?"

Sophie ran her eyes down the page. "Because they started fighting," she said. "About absolutely EVERYTHING—for Pete's sake—whether they were Protestant or Catholic—who liked England and who didn't—I don't even GET most of this stuff."

"Who are the bad guys?"

"Who can tell?" Sophie studied the page.

"There have to be bad guys if there's fighting. How do the good guys win if there's no bad guys?"

"I'm getting to that."

"Well, hurry up!" Zeke got up on his knees beside her and thumped the page with his chubby index finger.

"Okay, okay! Let's see—people live separate from people who don't believe like they do—like, behind cement walls and iron gates and stuff. People throw bombs over the walls—"

Sophie stopped and sucked in a breath. Did Darbie live like that? With burned-out houses all around her, like the book said?

"Spider-Man will save 'em from bombs!" Zeke cried.

"Don't start climbing the walls yet. There's more." Sophie repositioned her glasses. She felt herself frowning and ignored Zeke's new ascent up the side of the mattress. "It got REALLY ugly way back in 1969—I don't even know if Mama and Daddy were born by then. People were killing each other, Zeke. The British Army had to come up there and try to stop it."

Zeke stopped in mid-crawl across the bedspread. "You mean, like soldiers?"

"Yeah, right in front of their houses and stuff. They're still there!"

"Not after Spider-Man gets there!"

Zeke took a leap toward the dresser, but Sophie's mind was latched onto the image of Darbie, running past soldiers when she went to catch the bus for school. It made Sophie shiver.

The door opened just after Zeke hit the floor with a five-year-old thud.

"Hey, buddy, try to save the pieces, would you?" Daddy said. "So I can repair the floor after you fall through it." He looked at Sophie. "We're almost done—don't let Spider-Man get too carried away, okay?"

Colleen O'Bravo nodded, but her mind was far from the exploits of a small boy living out his daydreams. She had important things to attend to—like how to wash the feet of an Irish girl who had grown up with soldiers marching down her street, and trying to keep people from making bombs and throwing them into each other's neighborhoods.

After all, the great Irish doctor had given her the secret coded message. She had to treat her the way the Master, Jesus, had treated his friends.

When she woke up the next morning, Sophie knew exactly how she was going to do that. When she asked her mother,

Mama's eyes got all soft the way they did every Mother's Day when the three kids lined up with their made-in-school presents.

"I'll have everything ready," she said. She hugged the Ireland book Sophie handed to her. "Thanks for the information."

At school, Sophie told the Corn Flakes and Darbie that they had to meet at her house after school and come to a final decision, before Miss Blythe slapped "Twinkle, Twinkle, Little Star" on them Thursday. Fiona cornered Sophie at their lockers in the back of Mr. Denton's room and whispered, "You can't keep stuff from your best friend. I know you too well. What's really going to happen at your house?"

Sophie pulled some hair under her nose.

"Now I know something's going on!" Fiona's eyes drooped. "How come you're keeping this a secret from me?"

"I just want it to be a surprise," Sophie said. *Besides*, she added to herself, *you might try to talk me out of it.*

And when she saw Fiona slit her eyes toward Darbie as she slid into her seat in the classroom, Sophie knew she was right. This had to happen for more than just one reason.

The day dragged on like it was hauling three backpacks' worth of homework behind it—but finally they were all piling into the LaCroix's Suburban after sixth period and Mama was making sure everybody had called home for permission.

"I talked to your mom personally," Mama said to Darbie.

"She's not my ma," Darbie said between her teeth.

"Who is she?" Kitty said.

"Can you ever lay off?" Darbie said.

Sophie decided that qualified as eating the head off Kitty.

"How was everyone's day?" Mama sang out.

"Getting worse by the minute," Fiona whispered to Sophie. "This better be good."

It looked like it was going to be. The instant the group got to Sophie's family room, Sophie knew Mama had read the Ireland book cover to cover. There was a green table-cloth on the big square coffee table along with a white teapot with shamrocks on it, and a stack of tea bags all labeled Irish Breakfast Tea. Beside a plate of cloud-shaped biscuits was a vase full of tinted-green carnations and clover. Mama even had music playing that made Sophie want to dance the way they'd seen Darbie do for the Corn Pops.

"Welcome, Darbie," Mama said. "Sophie wanted to give you an Irish-American party. This might not be exactly the way it was in your home, but—"

"I love this!" Kitty said, with a Kitty-squeal. "Can I pour the tea?"

"Okay—I have to admit—this is pretty cool," Fiona said. Her eyes lit up like birthday-candle flames. "Let's all pick Irish names! I bet Sophie already has hers."

"Colleen O'Bravo," Sophie said. She smiled at Darbie. "Does that sound Irish?"

"No," Darbie said. "It sounds like some little-girlish thing you fancied out of the air." She looked at the tea things Mama had set up. "This isn't anything like Northern Ireland."

"Hello! Rude!" Fiona said.

But before Fiona could finish the step she started to take toward Darbie, Sophie was wedged between them, so close to Darbie she could see her nose hairs.

"It *is* little-girlish, Darbie!" Sophie said. "Because we are little girls—and all we're trying to do is make you feel like you have friends because that's what we do."

"Well, perhaps you are little girls," Darbie said. "But I am not. I never had a chance to be a little girl—and I don't even know HOW!"

Her eyes flashed down at Sophie just long enough for Sophie to see tears. And then Darbie turned and ran, slamming the front door behind her.

Seven

Mama sorted things out as only Mama could do. Within five minutes, Kitty's mom was picking her and Fiona up and taking them home, and Mama was on her way out to the Suburban with Darbie, who was shaking like a puppy.

"I just want to go home is all," she kept saying. "Please—let me go home."

It was way too hard to stay in the family room with the untouched Irish Breakfast Tea. Sophie flung herself facedown across her bed and was just starting to get Colleen O'Bravo into focus when Lacie threw herself down beside Sophie.

"How do you stand it when you get grounded?" she moaned.

Sophie frowned into the purple bedspread. "I just do."

"They aren't making me quit softball, but they grounded me for ten days! I'm already bored out of my skull!"

"It's not that bad," Sophie said. She brought her head up and rested it on her hand. "It gives me more time to come up with ideas for movies."

Lacie lifted her face, and Sophie expected an eye roll, but instead Lacie peered closely at her. "You know something?" she said. "Since you started making those films all the time, you hardly ever get grounded anymore. Weird."

"Yeah," Sophie said. "But I can't do a film right now, and I'm scared I'm going to get in trouble again."

"You don't even know what trouble is," Lacie said. She propped herself up on her elbows. "Not only did I get grounded for what happened at the retreat, but it'll probably get our youth leader in trouble too. Daddy's going to a meeting at church about it tonight. He says we might change churches if they don't start being more about God—but I love that church! That's where all my friends are!" She turned stormy eyes on Sophie. "I liked it better when you were the one getting in trouble all the time."

At least you're getting Mama and Daddy to yourself, Sophie thought. *I'm the one who needs them right now—not you!*

Lacie rolled onto her back and watched Sophie for a minute.

"I'm sorry," she said suddenly. "I didn't mean to make it sound like you were a total loser. I'm the loser at this point—I HATE this!"

She hauled herself off the bed and threw herself out of Sophie's room and into her own. Sophie could hear her crying through the wall.

It was the first time Sophie had ever thought she knew just how Lacie felt.

But I haven't time to go to her, Colleen O'Bravo thought. I have Darbie to think about now—and she's hurting worse than Lacie, she is. And there's the problem of the project too. I'm thinking it's time we went to the Master.

But Sophie had only just gotten Jesus' kind eyes into view when she heard the front door open. Mama was talking to someone, and it obviously wasn't Zeke. Her voice, trailing up the stairwell, was low and sad.

"Sophie?" she said. "Come on down—we have company."

By the time Sophie got downstairs, Mama was already in the family room—with Darbie and a lady who had her arm around Darbie so tightly she had to be her "ma."

"Shall I warm up the tea?" Mama said.

The lady looked at Darbie, who was staring at the floor and shaking her head. The second Sophie set her foot on the family room carpet, Darbie let go with a flood of tears that made no sound.

"Did I do something to hurt her feelings?" Sophie said to Darbie's ma.

"No, honey," the lady said. She didn't talk like Darbie at all. She sounded like someone who had been born and raised right there in Poquoson. She looked that way too, with her blonde hair flipped up everywhere and her frosty lipstick put on so perfectly it didn't go outside the lines of her lips.

Sophie looked at Mama for some magic words. Mama patted the sofa beside her and hugged Sophie's arm when she sat down.

"Darbie's pretty upset, but it isn't at you," Mama said. "Mrs. O'Grady is going to explain why."

"You can call me Aunt Emily," the lady said. She pronounced "aunt" like "ont." "That's what Darbie calls me."

Sophie had at least twenty-five questions raising their hands in her head, but she just nodded. She was afraid any word from her would start Darbie shaking again.

"I don't know how much you know about the Troubles in Northern Ireland," Aunt Emily said.

Sophie told her what she'd learned from the book, and Aunt Emily gave Mama a wide-eyed look. Even Darbie glanced up before she lowered her wet eyelashes toward the floor again.

"Sophie wanted to know everything she could about Darbie," Mama said.

"Then you'll understand Darbie's story, Sophie," Aunt Emily said. "Darbie's father—that would be my husband's brother—was very involved in trying to stop the fighting in Belfast in the 1980s. He was killed right after Darbie was born, just before the cease-fire was declared." She ran a manicured hand up and down Darbie's back. "He would have been so happy to see a move toward the peace he worked so hard for. There is still violence, but it was progress, and it had his fingerprints on it."

I bet Darbie doesn't even remember her dad, Sophie thought. As much as Daddy drove her nuts sometimes, she couldn't imagine never even knowing him.

"Darbie's mother carried on his work," Aunt Emily went on. "She helped start the Women's Coalition, which was very important in reaching the Belfast Agreement of 1998." Aunt Emily squeezed Darbie against her. "She was quite a lady, your mother, wasn't she?"

For the first time, Darbie lifted her face. Darbie was so close to Aunt Emily, Sophie was sure she probably went cross-eyed as she looked at her, but it seemed to stop her lips from trembling. She didn't move as Aunt Emily almost whispered the rest.

"And then, just six months ago, Darbie's mother died in a car accident. After growing up poor and without a father in the midst of so much violence, I think that was the hardest thing of all." She pulled Darbie's face into her chest and looked over her head at Sophie and Mama. "Harder than anything a little girl should have to go through."

Mama slipped her hand into Sophie's, and Sophie could feel her crying right down to her fingertips.

"My husband and I went to Northern Ireland and brought Darbie back here to live with us," Aunt Emily said. "I've been homeschooling her, and now that she has her bearings a little bit we thought it would be good for her to be in public school so she can make some friends."

Darbie turned her head and glanced at Sophie. Her eyes looked ashamed.

"She told me you have tried to include her," Aunt Emily said, "but it's so hard for her to trust people."

"Well, not only that," Mama said. "For heaven's sake, she hasn't lived the life the girls here have lived. No wonder she thought their group was 'little-girlish.'"

Aunt Emily nodded and went on into something Sophie didn't hear. Sophie could see so clearly in her mind Darbie locking all the doors and windows twenty times to keep out the people who hated her mother—and boiling the water for corned beef and cabbage while she waited for her ma to come home from her Coalition meeting, afraid to go out because she might be hit with a brick.

And praying that she wasn't riddled with bullets, the way her father was. If her mother was killed too, she wouldn't have anybody. Nobody to protect her from bombs and broken bottles being thrown. She could hear Darbie praying, "Jesus, please don't let them take my ma too—"

"Honey, are you all right?"

Sophie looked up at Aunt Emily through a blur of tears.

"I didn't mean to make you cry. I just wanted you to understand—"

"I do!" Sophie said. "And I hate it for her! I hate it for you, Darbie."

And then there was nothing else to say.

Not until Darbie slowly lifted herself out of her aunt's arms and shoved the tears from her cheeks with stiff fingers.

"I hate to cry," Darbie said. "I never cry." She whipped her face to meet Aunt Emily's. "But you were right—it feels good!"

After that, Darbie sobbed and sobbed, so hard that Mama and Sophie went into the kitchen to warm up the tea so she and Aunt Emily could be alone.

Mama stroked Sophie's cheek. "She says this is the first time she's seen Darbie cry since her mama died. This is a good thing."

"Is it okay if I tell Fiona and Kitty and Maggie?" Sophie said.

"I think you should ask Darbie," Mama said.

"I hope she says yes—because then they'd understand why she doesn't want to be friends with anybody here—why she ... like ... doesn't trust anybody." She gnawed at her lower lip. "Especially Fiona."

Mama poured hot water from the microwave into the teapot and looked at Sophie through the steam. "You know what, Soph? I think you've figured out what Darbie's parents were trying to do. They just wanted people to understand so they would stop fighting." She set down the water and folded her arms on the counter to look into Sophie's eyes. "Have you decided on anything for the showcase yet?"

Sophie shook her head. She'd forgotten all about that.

"What about helping all the kids understand about Darbie—if she approves it. Y'all are so good at acting things out."

"You would ask Miss Blythe to let us do a movie?" Sophie said.

Mama smiled her wispy smile and picked up the tea tray. "Who says you have to act it out on film?" she said.

Sophie trailed behind her to the family room, wailing out questions.

"But we never did it live before! What if we mess up? What if Kitty forgets her lines? She always forgets her lines!"

Mama turned to her just as they got to the door. "For heaven's sake, Dream Girl—use your imagination."

Darbie had stopped crying when they went in, and she was blowing her nose on a shamrock-covered paper napkin. She stuffed it into her pocket when she saw Sophie. "Do you think I'm completely gone in the head?" Darbie said.

"How about no!" Sophie said. "I think you're amazing—and not just like you're a specimen under a microscope."

"Excuse me?" Aunt Emily said.

"So if you hate this idea for our showcase, just tell me," Sophie said. "I can take it."

"Carry on, then," Darbie said.

Sophie glanced at Mama, got the nod, and told Darbie about the idea.

"It wouldn't be like using you," she said when she was almost out of breath. "It would be so other kids could understand."

Darbie leaned forward, her now-puffy eyes drilling into Sophie. "Would it get those ridiculous popettes to stop acting the maggot with me?" she said.

"The Corn Pops?" Sophie could feel a smile forming, because she was pretty sure what "acting the maggot" meant. "It might," she said.

"Then I say we stop foostering about and do it," Darbie said.

She stuck out her hand, and Sophie shook it. Darbie's fingers were hard and firm, like a grown-up's. It made Sophie feel sad for the little girl she never got to be.

Eight

Sophie and Darbie vowed to present their idea to the Corn Flakes the next morning before school. Sophie insisted they include Maggie so she wouldn't feel left out.

"We Corn Flakes take care of each other's feelings," Sophie told Darbie.

"Fair play!" Darbie said.

Sophie had a feeling that meant she was impressed.

The next day was March-rainy, so they met backstage — and early, in case the Corn Pops decided to come in and rehearse.

"They think they own the stage now," Kitty said when they were situated on the hay bales. "Hurry up, Sophie — tell us the idea before they come."

"I don't know why you couldn't have just told us over the phone," Fiona said. She pulled a Pop-Tart from her backpack and took a huge hunk out of it with her teeth.

No wonder she's grumpy this morning, Sophie thought. *She hasn't had breakfast.* It was obvious there was no new nanny yet.

While Fiona chewed sullenly, Sophie and Darbie unfolded the story of Darbie's life in Northern Ireland and what they wanted to do with it onstage.

"My dad said he would film it for us so we could still have a movie," Sophie said. "This is gonna be our *real*est one yet."

She wisped a smile over at Darbie, who gave her one back.

"We'll get it right down to the wee details," Darbie said.

"Wow."

They all turned to look at Maggie.

"I wish I was still in this group," she said.

For the first time that morning, Sophie saw Fiona's face light up. "Does the Corn Pops' dance stink?"

"No. It's way good. But *I* don't have anything to do with it. I'm making the costumes by myself. Me and my mom. And all the Corn Pops do is fight all the time." She shrugged. "Every one of them says they want to beat you guys for first prize—so you would think they would agree since they all want the same thing. But then they start yelling, and somebody is always crying." She looked at Kitty. "Willoughby cries more than you do."

"All right then," Fiona said, chin firm. "One thing we have going for us is unity. We can so beat them."

Sophie cut her eyes sideways at Darbie, who was studying Fiona like she was a textbook.

"Right," Sophie said slowly. "We'll make everybody understand about how it's stupid to fight over being different." She inserted a nod. "That's our mission."

"And we have only eight days to do it," Fiona said, though Sophie had the feeling Fiona hadn't even heard her. "We have to practice every day after school and the whole weekend."

"But not at your house," Kitty said. "Remember my dad."

"It wouldn't work anyway," Fiona said. "Not without a nanny for the brats. Okay, so who doesn't have annoying siblings running around to drive us nuts?"

"I don't," Darbie said. "You can come to my house."

Fiona tapped her bow of a mouth with her fingertip. "Where do you live?"

"What does that matter?" Darbie said.

For a moment, Fiona's eyes narrowed and nearly met at the bridge of her nose. Just as Sophie began to wriggle on top of her hay bale, Fiona shook her head. "I guess we don't have any other choice."

Sophie felt as if a shadow had just passed over the stage, although it lifted some when they found Miss Blythe in the hall and told her their plan. She pressed her jangling hand to her collarbone, closed her eyes, and said, "Brilliant. Absolutely brilliant." Then she told them they had to have a script for her by Monday.

"That is absolutely no problem," Fiona assured her. "Sophie and I have had a plethora of experience writing scripts."

"What's a 'plethora'?" Darbie said when Miss Blythe had sailed off.

"It means more than anybody else," Fiona said. She didn't have to say *including you*. Sophie could see it glinting in her gray eyes.

They started work at Darbie's house that very afternoon. After all, it was only four days until the script was due.

Darbie's aunt and uncle's place was right on the Poquoson River, a rambling, two-story house made of white boards that looked as if they'd just been painted. There were four boats of different sizes moored at the dock in the backyard.

"We aren't going to put a boat scene in this, are we?" Kitty asked, gazing nervously out the back window as she sipped the limeade that pretty, perky Aunt Emily had fixed for them—green to put them in an Irish mood, with real lime slices hooked on the sides of the glasses.

"We couldn't do that on a stage, Kitty," Sophie told her gently—before Fiona could get an eye roll in. She currently seemed to be looking for a chance to roll them around at somebody.

Darbie led them to a paneled room that was lined with books and had a telescope in the window—since, as she put it, her bedroom was in a "desperate condition." Sophie made a note to herself to include as many of Darbie's expressions as possible in the script. *I've already learned most of Fiona's words,* she thought. *Now I have all this new vocabulary.*

Fiona opened the Treasure Book and whipped out a pen. "Since Maggie isn't here, I'll write everything down. I think we should start the film—oops, play—where Darbie's a baby—"

"A little thing," Sophie put in.

"—and her father gets killed. Darbie could play her own mom and be holding a baby doll. Izzy has like a hundred of them—"

"But how will they know why my father was killed?" Darbie said.

"You mean background," Fiona said. She wafted the pen in the air with a flourish. "We'll just put that in the program for people to read. It would be too boring to tell it."

"Not the way Sophie does it," Darbie said.

Sophie was beginning to like the way Darbie pronounced her name—Soophie. She decided to ask Fiona and Kitty later to say it that way from now on.

"Tell them the way you told it to my aunt yesterday," Darbie said to Sophie.

"That's not how you do a play though," Fiona said. She tapped her chin with the end of the gel pen as if she were waiting for Darbie to get that so they could move on.

Sophie cocked her head at Fiona. "But somebody could be telling that at the front of the stage while Darbie's father was walking along, and then other people could come out and jump him—you know, like, what's that called?"

"You mean pantomime?" One side of Fiona's lip lifted.

"Then there aren't any lines to learn!" Kitty said. She took a happy slurp out of her limeade until the straw grumbled at the bottom of the glass.

"Why not do the whole lot of it that way?" Darbie said to Sophie. "We might take our turns narrating and the rest could be in pantomime."

"No offense, Darbie," Fiona said. "But we don't do our films that way."

"But this isn't the flicks," Darbie said.

"Does that mean movies?" Kitty said.

"Yes."

"I like that. Let's start calling our movies the 'flicks'!"

"Would you please stay on task?" Fiona snapped at her, pen jittering on the table. "Now we only have three and a *half* days to get this done."

"All the more reason to do it in narration and pantomime," Darbie said.

Fiona looked at Sophie, shaking her head. "Explain it to her, would you, Soph? You're, like, the only one she understands."

Sophie reached for the end of her hair to make a mustache, and then tossed it over her shoulder. "I like the idea," she said. "I can just see it in my mind."

"Well, the rest of us can't," Fiona said.

"I can," Kitty said. "Darbie, do you think you have any more of that limeade stuff?"

"Kit-teee!" Fiona said.

"This is a class idea!" Darbie said. "I'll fetch us some more to drink."

When Kitty had skipped off after Darbie, Fiona stared hard at Sophie.

"Why are you letting her be the boss of everything?" Fiona said. "You're the director, and she's usurping your authority."

Okay, so that was one Sophie hadn't heard before. "I don't think I AM the director this time," Sophie said. "This is Darbie's story, so she knows more about it than we do."

Fiona yanked her hair out of her face. "She has never made a film before — or done any acting at all, I bet. You have to take control if she starts to mess this up, Sophie — or we'll never beat the Corn Pops."

"She won't make a bags of it! And besides, that's not why — "

"Come here, you guys!" Kitty squealed from down the hall. "Darbie's got posters we can use and everything! This is going to be way cool!"

It WAS cool. Darbie's uncle had signs that had actually been on walls during "the Troubles" — saying things like "Disband the RUC," whatever that meant. There was so much Sophie still didn't understand about the Troubles. They also had pictures of Darbie's old school and house in Northern Ireland so they could set up the stage exactly the way it was for each scene. Fiona argued that it would take too much time changing furniture every other minute, but Sophie and Darbie figured out a way to use the same few chairs and one table for every scene and just change things like flowers in a vase or a pile of schoolbooks. Aunt Emily told them she was impressed. She said she did some theater when she was in college, and that's exactly what they used to do.

So it only seemed to make sense that Darbie and Sophie would write the script and hand the scenes to Fiona and Kitty to figure out what Aunt Emily called the "set changes." Sophie told them to be sure to talk in the new theater language Aunt Emily was teaching them.

Kitty was amazingly good at it. Sophie couldn't tell whether Fiona was or not because she spent most of the time scowling at the Treasure Book while she wrote things down. Still, by Saturday afternoon the whole script was written, which meant they didn't have to meet on Sunday.

But Saturday night, Darbie called and asked Sophie if she could come over the next day anyway and make sure everything was perfect before they handed it in to Miss Blythe on Monday.

That day was Sophie's favorite day of work—because as she and Darbie took turns reading the narration and walking through the scenes of pantomime, it all became real.

Sophie clutched at her chest as she hid behind a "counter" in a chipper—a fish and chips shop—being little Darbie, while angry men dragged the owner out into the street, yelling at him because he wasn't welcome in the neighborhood.

She felt a lump in her throat as she waved good-bye to her ma, who was going off to another peace talk someplace far away.

And she cried real tears as she put flowers next to a "headstone" on that same ma's grave.

"You *have* to play me when we perform this, Sophie," Darbie said—handing Sophie a box of Kleenex. "I can't even be me like you can!"

"Then you have to play your ma," Sophie said. "Because you're the only one who can make me cry like that."

That would mean, of course, that Kitty and Fiona would take turns reading and playing all the other parts.

"Fiona won't fancy that," Darbie said.

"You mean she won't like it?" Sophie said. "She'll love it! She's very versatile—you know, like she can play any role." Sophie nodded thoughtfully at the script. "We should have her put more big words in the narration too."

Darbie agreed. Fiona didn't.

Before school on Monday, Sophie told Fiona everything as the four of them half ran down the hall to find Miss Blythe.

"You don't have time to do it before we give it to her right now," Sophie said breathlessly. "But you can do it later."

"What if I don't want to do it at all?" Fiona said. She slowed to a walk, so that Sophie had to cut back her pace too. She stared at Fiona.

"Why not?" Sophie said.

"Because it's not my script," Fiona said. "It's yours and Darbie's. And now you want me to come in and fix it for you so you'll sound smarter."

Sophie squinted at her. "I don't get it."

Fiona rolled her eyes and sighed and shook her head.

"It's so obvious, Sophie," she said. "If you don't know, I'm sure not going to tell you."

Sophie couldn't get her mouth to move. She was still just gawking at Fiona, as Darbie would say, when Kitty and Darbie ran back to them. Kitty jumped right up on Fiona's back, piggy back style.

"We gave it to Miss Blythe!" she said, arms locked around Fiona's neck.

"She's going to love it, so she is!" Darbie said. It was the first time Sophie had ever heard a giggle in Darbie's voice.

Fiona shook Kitty from her back and kept her eyes on Sophie. "If she doesn't," she said, "don't expect me to fix it."

As it turned out, Miss Blythe didn't think it needed "fixing" at all. She sailed right over to their group's table in arts class with the script and went on and on about the creativity and the sensitivity and every other "ivity" they had managed to get in there, all the while squiggling her fingers in the air with punctuation marks Sophie had never seen before.

Kitty and Darbie beamed. Fiona sulked. Sophie closed her eyes and tried to imagine Jesus so she could beg him for an answer to this new mess.

It seems like I just get one thing worked out, she said to him in her mind, *and something else goes wrong. Now what do I do?*

She peeked at Fiona, who was still looking at Miss Blythe with lead in her eyes.

And why is Fiona making this so hard?

Sophie wanted to drag her out into the hallway and eat the head off her, as Darbie would say. That's how mad she was.

It was hard to keep from showing that over the next three days as the group rehearsed. Darbie told Sophie that Fiona had a "right puss on her, she did," but Sophie was determined not to let Fiona's pouting spoil their presentation. Every time Fiona shrugged when they asked for her opinion, or read the narration like a first grader in a reading group, or walked through a scene as if she were a stick instead of a "bitter peeler" — the Irish term for policeman — Sophie just chewed at her lip and kept going.

Until Wednesday, just three days before the performance. And then she couldn't hold it back any longer.

Nine

The group was rehearsing that Wednesday after school at Darbie's, using her back deck as the stage. They had all their tables and chairs—their set pieces, Aunt Emily told them—and the small stuff like flowers and teacups—their props, Aunt Emily said—everything lined up perfectly backstage. There was a copy of the script for each of them, and they were even wearing their costumes. They wore blue jeans and white T-shirts so they could put other things on top—aprons and hats and Sophie's black velvet cape, which she wore as Darbie going to her ma's gravestone. Kitty had surprised them with that scathingly brilliant idea.

Everything would have been perfect—except that Fiona was being such the Puss Face, as Darbie whispered to Sophie, that she would hardly speak to anyone, and when she did, every word squeezed out between her teeth like the last of the glue coming out of the tube.

"The audience won't be able to hear you if you don't talk louder," Sophie said during one of Fiona's tight-jawed narrations.

"I don't see any audience," Fiona said.

"There will be one," Sophie said. "We have to pretend they're there."

78

"They'll all be asleep anyway," Fiona said. "So what difference does it make?"

Over on stage left Kitty's forehead puckered up. "Why will they be asleep?"

"They won't," Sophie said. She looked hard at Fiona. "Let's do that part again."

It was that way all through rehearsal, which made it hard for Sophie to concentrate on being Darbie. Instead of imagining that the wadded-up brown lunch bags Fiona and Kitty were throwing were stones being pelted at Darbie by mean kids, she saw the Fruit Loops drooling and snoring in the back of the room and the Corn Pops dozing off nearby. *The audience wouldn't go to sleep if YOU weren't so boring!* she wanted to shout at Fiona. The way Fiona walked around all stiff during the throw-rocks-at-Darbie scene made Kitty act like a robot too.

But at least Darbie's giving it her best, Sophie thought. During the part where Darbie's mother died on the street next to her smashed car with Darbie/Sophie at her side, Darbie touched Sophie's face like a real mother would, and Sophie burst into tears.

"That'll wake the audience up," Fiona said. "They'll be guffawing all over the place."

Darbie sat straight up and glared at her. "What does that mean?"

"Throwing up?" Kitty said.

Fiona shook her head. "Laughing themselves into oblivion. That is so corny."

"Her mother died!" Sophie said. "I'm supposed to cry!"

"It sounds fake," Fiona said. She studied her fingernails. "I think we should take that scene out. We need to get some humor in."

"Humor!" Sophie said.

She could feel Darbie stiffening beside her. "What's such a gas about this?"

"That means 'what's funny,'" Sophie said.

"Nothing," Fiona said. "That's the point. The Corn Pops are going to be entertaining the audience. We're going to be making them wish they were having a tooth pulled or something."

"We'll entertain them too!" Sophie said. Looking up, she could see right up Fiona's flaring nostrils.

"Right," Fiona said. "They'll be laughing at us."

"Will they, Sophie?" Kitty said.

"No, they will not." Sophie's words came out as squeezed-tight as Fiona's. "Not unless Fiona keeps on making a bags of it."

"Acting the maggot," Darbie mumbled.

"I knew it," Fiona squeezed back at Sophie. "I knew you would turn all this into my fault. But I'm not the one. I didn't have anything to do with this. You and Darbie planned it all, and then you're all telling me and Kitty what to do!" Fiona shoved her hair out of her face with the side of her hand. "I'm so not your little slave. If you don't start listening to me, I'm going to find another group to be in. And don't think I won't!"

She planted her hands on her hips and lowered her face so that she was slitting her eyes right into Sophie's like a pair of knives. Sophie felt her own slashing back.

"You're being selfish, Fiona," she said. "We're doing this for Darbie — not for you!"

There was a stinging silence. Somewhere in the middle of it, Fiona tore her script into confetti and stormed into the house. Nobody followed her.

After a few minutes, Aunt Emily came out, mouth in a grim line, and suggested they call it a day and let everybody cool off. Kitty looked more than happy to escape.

"I don't think this was a good idea at all, Sophie," Darbie said when Kitty was gone. She tucked her swingy hair behind both ears, and Sophie could see a red rim forming around each eye.

"It's the best idea ever," Sophie said. "It's class. I just don't think Fiona gets what we're trying to do."

Darbie pulled her lips into a thin line, the way a grown-up would. "If she doesn't, nobody will."

"Then we totally have to do it so they all will." She knew she was sounding like Kitty, but there was no other way to sound. She felt so much younger than Darbie all of a sudden.

"I won't be made to look like an eejit," Darbie said. Her eyes went hard as stones. "I'll take a bad grade before I'll be laughed at."

Sophie opened her mouth—and then she closed it again, because now she couldn't promise Darbie that the entire audience wouldn't fall right out of their chairs.

Aunt Emily invited Sophie to stay for supper, and she and Darbie's uncle Patrick spent the whole time, as far as Sophie was concerned, turning themselves inside out to make the girls laugh. But the last thing Sophie wanted to do was "guffaw."

By the time Aunt Emily took her home, Mama and Daddy had already left for a meeting at church, and Zeke was asleep. Sophie curled up on her bed and tried to sort out whether to imagine Colleen O'Bravo, get Jesus in her mind, or just camp outside Mama and Daddy's bedroom door until they got home and beg them to let her see Dr. Peter. She was ready to try all three when Lacie tapped on the door and let herself in before Sophie could even tell her to go away.

"I am so bored!" Lacie said as she sprawled across Sophie's bed just like she'd done every day since she'd been grounded.

"Make yourself at home," Sophie said in a dry voice.

"I've done all my homework. I've studied for my geography test twelve times. I've written letters to everybody I ever knew in Houston—I mean letters—not even email. You'd think they'd at least let me get on the Internet."

"No, you wouldn't," Sophie said. "You're grounded."

"Really, Einstein?" Lacie sighed. "So what are you doing?"

Sophie pulled her script out of her backpack. "I'm trying to figure out what to do about our play."

"Another film?" Lacie said. "I don't know what you'd do if you had real problems."

"I do!" Sophie said. "This is for a school project. Everybody's parents are going to be there, and if Fiona doesn't get her act together, I'm going to have to transfer to another school or something."

"Let me see that, Drama Queen," Lacie said. She snatched the script from Sophie's hand.

"If you're going to make me feel like an eejit, I will eat the head off you."

"Whatever that means." Lacie moved her eyes across the page. Sophie flopped back against her pillows and tried to think what Colleen O'Bravo would do if she had a sister. She didn't, of course. She was an orphan without siblings, ever since the Troubles—

"Huh," Lacie said.

"Just give it back," Sophie said. She stuck her hand out, but Lacie waved her away, her eyes still glued to the page.

"Who wrote this?" Lacie said.

"I did—well, Darbie and I did. She's Irish."

"Is this like her story or something?" Lacie said.

"Yes—which is why I don't want you laughing at it. All those things really happened to her."

"Dude—it's horrible."

82

"It isn't horrible! Miss Blythe said it was a good script—"

"I'm not talking about the script—I'm talking about what happened to this Darbie chick. How could a person go through something like that?" Lacie turned the page and after a moment she looked up at Sophie, who was now breathing like the spin cycle on the washing machine. "This is good, Soph. You sure you guys didn't have somebody helping you?"

"Yes," Sophie said. She felt a smile starting to form, and then she scowled up at the ceiling. "I wish Fiona thought it was good. She says we're going to get laughed out of the school."

"I guess it could get cheesy when you act it out," Lacie said.

"Only if *she* keeps acting like she hates it," Sophie said. "She's supposed to be my best friend, and she's being all stupid and making a bags of the whole thing and messing everything up. Darbie doesn't deserve that."

"Did I miss the part where you started speaking another language?" Lacie tossed the script on the bedspread and turned on her side, cheek in hand as she leaned on her elbow. "Okay—let me get this straight. You and Darbie wrote the script. You spent all day Sunday at Darbie's house. You ate dinner at Darbie's house tonight. But Fiona's your best friend."

"Yeah," Sophie said. "So?"

"Du-uh!" Lacie said. "It doesn't take a genius to figure out that Fiona's feeling left out because you're paying all this attention to Darbie. Get a clue, Soph."

"But we already went through this with Maggie when we were doing our science project! Fiona knows I can be friends with other people and still be her best friend."

"But back then, every other word that came out of your mouth wasn't 'Maggie.' Besides, you and Maggie and Fiona and—what's that little whiny child's name?"

"Kitty."

"Ya'll are all friends with each other. How does Irish Girl fit in?"

Sophie considered that as she poked at a tiny hole in the bedspread. "Darbie likes Fiona okay — but I think she knows Fiona doesn't like her that much."

Lacie sat up, legs crossed in front of her. "Okay, so two things are different. One — you didn't spend every spare minute with Maggie and leave Fiona out, and two — Maggie was part of the group, and Darbie isn't. She's not a — what do you guys call yourselves?"

"Corn Flakes."

Sophie's throat felt thick, and it was hard to breathe. She hadn't meant to hurt Fiona, but the way Lacie described it Sophie might as well have punched her best friend in the heart.

"Fiona probably hates me now!" she said.

Lacie put up both hands. "Okay, don't go flipping out on me. For once in your life, listen to a little advice from me — hello, I've been there."

Sophie doubted that, but she nodded. Anything to keep from losing Fiona, which was suddenly more important than the showcase or Colleen O'Bravo or even her video camera.

"Look," Lacie said, "you have to make Fiona feel like she's important again."

"The only way to do that is to drop Darbie," Sophie said.

"Are you going to listen to me or what?"

Sophie gave her another glum nod.

"You call Fiona up and tell her she's your best friend in the world and you want to hear why she thinks the script is lame."

"But it isn't."

"No, duh. But just listen to her and make her feel like you're taking it all in — and then you tell her she's the only one who can make it work."

"That's not true."

"Sure it is. If she keeps 'making bags out of it' or whatever, it is going to bomb. You said that yourself."

Sophie squinted through her glasses. "You think that'll work?"

"Trust me. Do it right now. I'll get the phone—at least that'll give me an excuse to hold it in my hand. I'm going into telephone withdrawal. I'm going to forget how to use one."

Before Sophie could even think about it, Lacie punched in Fiona's number and handed the phone to Sophie.

"I'll stay here in case you need any coaching," Lacie said. "Hold it out so I can hear."

You really are bored, Sophie thought. But for the first time since Fiona had ripped up her script, Sophie felt a little sparkle of hope. When Fiona answered the phone, she launched right in.

But before she could even get out the words, "I am so sorry about what happened this afternoon"—with Lacie nodding at her side—Fiona said, "Stop. Just stop."

"I was just—" Sophie said.

"If it's about the showcase thing, don't waste your time."

"But I really want to hear—"

"Forget it," Fiona said. "The Corn Pops still need another dancer. I'm auditioning for them tomorrow."

"No!" Sophie said.

Lacie put her fingers in her ears.

"I don't care if everybody laughs at me when I'm just being my weird self," Fiona said. "But I don't want them laughing if I'm doing something totally lame that isn't me. Besides—"

There was a pause. Lacie nudged Sophie.

"What?" Sophie said. "It doesn't have to be lame—I want to hear your ideas."

"I can't get a bad grade," Fiona said. "I'm the one who made sure you got good grades so you could have your camera. But now that you don't listen to me, you're going down. And I'm not going down with you."

It was abruptly silent. When a dull drone sounded in Sophie's ear, Lacie took the phone from her and pushed the button.

"She hung up, Soph," she said. "She just flat hung up on you."

Ten

Sophie stared at the phone, which was still in Lacie's hand.

"That was just wrong," Lacie said, flipping her ponytail. "If she's going to be that way about it, you don't need her for a friend."

"No—I do!" Sophie said. "It's all my fault!"

Lacie shook her head, but when the sound of Mama and Daddy coming through the kitchen made its way up the stairs, she was out the door in mid-shake.

"What happened?" Sophie heard her call down over the banister.

"We need to talk," Daddy called back up.

Sophie felt herself folding in as she got up and closed her door. *There goes another hour or two*, she thought.

In fact, it wasn't even a minute or two before Lacie was bellowing, "I don't want to go to another church! You're taking me away from my friends! I'm the middle school youth group president!"

Colleen O'Bravo perched the green hat atop her head and crumpled beneath its brim. "She'll eat the heads off of them for sure," she said to herself. "And it will not do a bit of good. When Ma and Da make up their minds—"

Sophie's thoughts trailed off. Colleen wasn't much help right now. Sophie was losing her best friend, and it was going to take more than imagination to get her back.

"I want Dr. Peter!" she whispered to the walls.

What would he say? She closed her eyes and pictured him on the window seat in his office, face pillow in hand, squinting through his glasses with twinkly blue eyes.

I read the Bible story, Sophie said to him in her mind. *And it helped me with Darbie. But Fiona—*

She could see Dr. Peter wrinkling his nose, pushing up his glasses. *No 'But Fiona,' Loodle*, he would say. *It's in the Bible. It's truth. Love her the way Jesus loves his friends.*

Sophie was about to kick her feet—rather than even think about washing them or anybody else's—when the phone jangled beside her. She snatched it up, the word "Fiona!" already on her lips.

But it was Darbie, jabbering like the words couldn't come out fast enough. "You haven't a clue who just called me! It was Fiona—and she reefed me!"

Sophie didn't even have to ask if that was the same as eating the head off her.

"She told me she was going to audition for the Corny Pops," Darbie went on. "Now what are we going to do? We'll surely make a bags of doing our show without her! This is desperate!"

"You know it!" Sophie said. "We have to get her back is all—I know you'll hate this idea, but I'm trying to figure out how I'm supposed to love her like Jesus. What I mean is—"

"I know all about that," Darbie said.

"You do?" Sophie said.

"Don't be thinking it isn't hard to love some blaggard who's just left your garden in flitters bolting through with his evil signs—or worse. I'm quite the expert on doing what the Lord says even when you'd rather be hanged. I've been doing it for ages."

Sophie sat up straighter on the bed. "You mean, like washing people's feet, sort of?"

"I know that story. And the one about the lady who wiped Jesus' feet with her *hair*."

Sophie barely took time to notice that Darbie pronounced Jesus, "Jaysus." She could only gawk at the phone.

"My ma and me, we always talked about the Bible stories—we would never have been able to carry on without them." Darbie's voice dropped. "My aunt and uncle don't go to church—and it's murder without it."

Sophie finally found her voice, and it came out squeaky-nervous. "You know the foot-washing story then?"

"I do."

"Well—we have to love Fiona like that. You know, wash her feet. Only I don't know how."

"It isn't difficult," Darbie said. "Bowl. Towel. Water."

"You mean, really wash her feet?" Sophie said. Her voice was squealing up into dog-world.

"That's what the story says. And you know what else it says, of course."

"No," Sophie said.

"Fetch your Bible, then," Darbie said.

But before Sophie could even reach for hers, the door opened and Daddy stuck his head in. The skin under his eyes was long. "Lights out, Soph," he said. "We'll talk tomorrow. Deal?"

Sophie nodded. When the door closed, she whispered to Darbie, "I have to go."

"Read the entire story," Darbie whispered back. "The part where he gives out to them—you know, gets in their faces, as you Americans say. Sometimes that's love too, my ma always told me, mostly when she was giving out to me about something I did wrong. Oh — and I'll bring the pitcher tomorrow."

"For what?" Sophie said.

"For the water. And let's do it in the corner of the play yard. I don't fancy having every eejit in the school gawking at us."

Sophie's mind was whirling when she hung up, but she reached for her Bible and her flashlight and tented herself under the covers.

Jesus loved them by getting in their faces? Sophie thought. *Sounds like something Daddy would say* — *"Soph, I'm doing this for your own good."*

Chewing at her hair, Sophie read the story three more times, searching for a place where Jesus — how had Darbie said it? — gave out to the disciples.

Okay, so I'm Luke, she thought, *and Jesus is being all nice and washing everybody's feet, and then he gets in our faces.* Sophie sat up and pretended that Jesus was back at his place at the table, leaning across to talk to them all. Sophie/Luke squinted back to see him. Jesus' voice was getting firmer; it was as if she could almost press her hand against his words.

"I tell you the truth," he said, *"no servant is greater than his master, nor is a messenger greater than the one who sent him. Now that you know these things, you will be blessed if you do them."*

Sophie tried to hear it again, with Jesus using an even sterner voice, like he wanted to make sure they got it. She couldn't quite remember the exact words. In her head it was, "If you understand what I'm saying to you, then act like it."

Sophie/Luke scrunched up his face as he tried to get it. As always, his teacher's eyes were kind even though he was stern, and he felt himself breathing deep in his chest. *He expects me*

90

to love and love and love some more, Sophie/Luke thought. He watched the faces of his friends glow in the half darkness. The Master Jesus was telling them what they had to do. But he wasn't getting all yelly and making them feel like — eejits. "This is what I have to do," Sophie/Luke told himself. "I have to make people understand, only with love."

By then, Sophie's eyes felt sandy, and she burrowed farther under the bedspread with the flashlight still in her hand.

Darbie knows about "Jaysus" too, she thought as she fell asleep. *What a CLASS discovery.*

Mama didn't even question why Sophie wanted to borrow a bowl and a towel to take to school. She bagged them up so Sophie could carry them on the bus without bopping anybody in the head, and as Sophie went for the door she said to her, "I'm sorry we haven't been much help to you, Dream Girl. But Daddy and I are going to make special time for you tonight."

As good as that sounded, Sophie couldn't think about it right then. She met Darbie at school just as Aunt Emily was dropping her off, and they waited like crouched tigers for Maggie and Kitty to appear. Sophie knew Fiona would be the last one to get there since, without a nanny, it was probably a zoo at her house in the mornings. That was fine, because it took a few minutes to explain the foot washing to Kitty and Maggie.

"I don't get it," Maggie said, her voice flat. "What if her feet aren't dirty?"

"It isn't about dirt," Sophie said patiently. "It's about showing Fiona that I love her and I respect her, but she can't just go off and pout."

Maggie shrugged. "So why don't you just tell her?"

"I tried that," Sophie said — less patiently. "She wouldn't listen — but this will get her attention."

"How do you know?" Maggie said.

Darbie gave a soft grunt. "Wouldn't it get yours?"

"I think it sounds cool!" Kitty said. "Will you do mine?"

"Fiona first," Sophie said.

"Since she's the one bolting off to join up with the Pop Corns," Darbie said.

Kitty would have died of the giggles if the Buntings' black SUV hadn't squealed up to the front of the school just then.

"Go out to your places, okay?" Sophie said.

Sophie hurried to grab Fiona the second her foot emerged from the car. Fiona slammed the door against the chaos inside the vehicle and tried to wriggle past her.

"No way," Sophie said to her as she dragged her away from the car door. "I'm going to love you whether you like it or not."

Somehow Sophie got her to the play yard, where the other girls were kneeling in the far corner, their backs to the rest of the Great Marsh Elementary world.

"I don't have time for this," Fiona said. They were the first words she'd spoken. "I have to go audition."

"You have to do this first," Sophie said. She hoped her eyes were Jesus-kind, because her voice was coming out in a very UN-Jesus way. He would never sound like a mom about to smack her kids in the cookie aisle at the Farm Fresh.

"Sit," Maggie said to Fiona when she and Sophie got to the corner. She pointed to a folded-up jacket placed on the ground for her bum.

Sophie sucked in a breath, but Fiona took a seat. *Good thing she can't resist a mystery*, Sophie thought.

Sophie got on her knees facing Fiona while Darbie poured water from the pitcher into the bowl and Kitty and Maggie took off Fiona's shoes—with only a halfway protest from Fiona. Sophie took off her jean jacket and wrapped a big beach towel around her waist.

"I get it," Fiona said. "You're going to stick my foot in that water—although why I can't even fathom."

"Because I love you, that's why," Sophie said. She cradled Fiona's heel in her palm and she could see her own hands shaking. Her voice was barely coming out at all. She was sure Jesus hadn't been this scared that it wasn't going to work.

"I want to serve you," Sophie said. "Not yell at you and make you feel left out." She leaned down and swept some water over Fiona's toes. "You're my best friend and I really want to hear your ideas."

Fiona seemed to be staring at the water bubbles. She didn't say a word.

"I'm sorry too," Darbie said. "It was diabolical of me not to consider your feelings."

"That must mean really terrible," Kitty muttered to Maggie.

Sophie pulled Fiona's feet out of the bowl and rested them on the towel across her lap. "Please don't go join up with the Corn Pops," she said as she dried between Fiona's toes. "We need you. I'll be a better friend, I promise."

Fiona finally looked up at her, forehead bunched into folds. "I don't know," she said.

"What's not to know?" Maggie said. "She apologized. She said she wants to serve you. Now you accept and it's done."

"Just because she washed my feet?" Fiona said.

"Can you ever stop being a hard chaw?" Darbie said. "She's groveling for you, and you're wanting more! I never saw such an ungrateful—"

"Don't yell!" Kitty said, just before she burst into tears.

"You sound like the Corn Pops," Maggie said. "I get enough of this at rehearsal."

"Maybe I'll just go be a Corn Pop!" Fiona said. "At least I know how they feel about me."

"Are you gone in the head?" Darbie said. "Sophie just told you—"

"Just stop! Everybody STOP!" Sophie's voice practically squeaked out of her ears as she struggled to her feet. The bowl turned over, and the water hurried toward the fence in rivulets. Nobody even looked at it. "We're the Corn Flakes," she said when they were quiet. "We take care of each other's feelings. And that means everybody. We don't act like this. Now just—stop."

She snatched up her jacket and hugged it around her, but she knew her shivers weren't from the cold. Even her voice was shaky as she said, "This is what we have to do. We have to stop fighting and we have to work together. If we don't, we're going to mess up our whole showcase—and the whole Corn Flakes."

"Nuh-uh!" Kitty said.

"Yuh-huh," Maggie said. "The Corn Pops' dance is, like, professional, but right now they can hardly stand each other."

"You don't even know how lucky you are to have friends like you do," Darbie said. "I had to leave all mine behind." She straightened her shoulders. "I can go off my nut sometimes, but I'll try not to eat the head off anyone again—you have my word."

Kitty whimpered. Sophie thought she said something like, "Pleeeeze, Fiona."

Fiona flipped her hair out of her face and looked at Maggie. "So the Corn Pops' dance is spectacular, huh?"

"They'll win," Maggie said.

For the first time in what felt to Sophie like centuries, Fiona's gray eyes flickered with interest. Her mouth came unbunched, and she gave a little bow of a smile. "Oh, no, they will *not* win," she said. She turned to Darbie. "Okay—it's over.

No more fighting. We are going to make this the BEST performance that ever was. Whatever it takes."

Darbie blinked for a second. "All right, then. Fair play," she said. Her voice was careful. "After school at my house? No foostering about?"

"No foostering," Fiona said. "I'm serious."

"I won't fooster, either," Kitty said.

The bell rang, and Maggie and Kitty and Darbie picked up the remains of the foot washing. Fiona tucked her arm through Sophie's and steered her toward the building.

Sophie felt strangely stiff beside her. Fiona had said she wanted to win the showcase—beat the Corn Pops. But that wasn't really the mission. Besides that, Fiona had never said she was sorry.

"Boppa says I'm insecure and I need to get over it," Fiona said. Her voice was sunny, as if they had not had a shouting match just five minutes before. "I guess I shouldn't have told you that I was going to audition for the Corn Pops. I called Julia and set it up, but I was never really going to do it. Boppa about ate the head off me when he heard me on the phone with her."

Then I washed your feet for nothing? Sophie wanted to say. She felt herself going even more rigid.

"You know what, Soph?" Fiona said.

Sophie shook her head.

"Sometimes I really want to know how you can be so good all the time." She pulled Sophie's arm closer. "I'm glad we're okay again."

Sophie nodded—but she wondered if they really were.

Eleven

Just as Darbie and Fiona had both promised, there were no more "ructions," as Darbie called them, while the group worked during every possible second on Thursday and Friday to make their play the best thing anyone had ever seen—at least at Great Marsh Elementary. It seemed to make Darbie happy that they were finally doing justice to her life story, and Kitty, of course, was happy because everybody else was happy.

But Sophie still had an unsettled feeling inside her about Fiona. Even during her special time with Mama and Daddy on Thursday night, while they ate yogurt and Mama's homemade granola in the kitchen, she couldn't quite explain it.

"All Fiona wants to do is win," she told them, "and our mission is to make people understand how horrible it can be if they fight and are violent—you know, like in Northern Ireland."

Daddy pulled his upper half out of the refrigerator, holding a can of whipped cream. "Why can't you do both?" he said. "Win and educate at the same time."

"Besides," Mama said, "I think it's what you and the other Corn Flakes are learning from all this that's really important. You're really being mature."

96

Daddy squirted a tall pile of whipped cream on his granola-topped yogurt and finished with a dot on Sophie's nose. "You're a winner no matter what happens, Soph. I wish it was this easy with your sister right now."

Sophie soaked that in for a second, waiting for a warm feeling to fill her up. But being praised over Lacie didn't do it for her like she'd always dreamed it would.

"We're changing churches, aren't we?" she said.

"We are," Mama said. "But I think it's going to be a good thing."

"Lacie doesn't think so."

"Right now, Lacie doesn't think — period." Daddy shook the whipped cream can again. "You don't look like you're about to pitch a fit over it though, Soph. I appreciate that."

"I don't have friends there like she does," Sophie said.

"You will at our new church. At least one." Mama grinned at Daddy. "Should I tell her?"

"Nah — make her beg."

"Da-ad!" Sophie snatched up the can and pointed it in his direction.

His hands flew up. "I'll tell you anything you want to know. Just don't shoot."

"Who's at the new church that I know?" Sophie said.

"A cute little man with glasses," Mama said. "He teaches Bible study to your age group."

"Dr. Peter?" Sophie said. "Go way outta that!"

"It's not a bit of a horse's hoof. I'm telling you the truth."

Daddy looked from one of them to the other, a mustache of whipped cream under his nose. "Why don't I understand a thing you women are saying?" he said.

Mama patted his arm. "You'd have to have a bit of the Irish in you," she said.

On Friday during arts class, each group went into the cafeteria-turned-auditorium to do its presentation privately for Miss Blythe, so she could make sure they were ready for a real audience. Sophie's group was scheduled to go last.

"Miss Blythe is saving the best for the end," Fiona whispered as they waited, dry-mouthed, backstage with their set pieces and props.

"She wants a dramatic finish," Darbie said.

"I have to go to the bathroom," Kitty said.

Sophie put her hands out and the Corn Flakes and Darbie grabbed on, and Sophie prayed. "Help us do what you did, Jesus, and that's help people understand."

"And please help us win," Fiona said.

"Amen," Kitty said.

"Are you ready, actors?' Miss Blythe called from in front of the stage.

Sophie tried to brush away the nagging Fiona-thought and gave Kitty a little push to go out and start the narration.

"Let's do it perfect," Fiona said.

"Perfect" didn't totally describe their performance for Miss Blythe. Kitty lost her place twice when she was reading the narration, and Fiona forgot to put out a chair for one of the scenes, and Sophie couldn't quite get the tears out at the "graveside." But when they were finished, Miss Blythe stood up and shouted, "Bravo! Brav-O!"

"I bet she didn't do that for the Corn Pops," Fiona whispered. Sophie could see the triumphant gleam in her eyes even in the dark behind the curtain. Sophie felt a bit victorious herself. Maybe, like Daddy said, they could educate AND win.

And then she looked at Darbie, who was twisting her mouth up as she looked at Fiona, like she was trying not to say out loud what she was thinking. But Sophie knew what it was. Fiona herself still didn't get it yet. Was there any chance that the other kids would?

It was hard, though, on Saturday not to think about the possibility of the entire audience standing up, calling out "Bravo!" The more the cheers and applause went through Sophie's head, the more she dreamed that the stage curtains were going to open up to the Corn Flakes' secret world, and other kids were finally going to understand about how stupid it was to hate and fight. She tried not to let herself add in a vision of herself accepting first prize with her fellow cast members and waving to Mama and Daddy in the front row and seeing them beam with pride. But that seemed to be the ONLY thing Fiona could think about.

She called four times on Saturday, just to assure Sophie that they were so going to blow everyone else away. Darbie called twice to ask Sophie to convince her that things were going to be "quite different" after their performance, what with the Corn Pops and Fruit Loops no longer "acting the maggot" because they would now be educated. She was still having trouble believing it. Kitty called only once, and Sophie couldn't tell whether she was giggling or crying. She was definitely Kitty-nervous.

Sophie wasn't very nervous — not with Daddy having flowers delivered to the house for her, and Mama fixing her an herbal bath and playing Irish music while she French-braided Sophie's hair, and even Lacie coming out of her church misery long enough to give her a card that said, "I'm actually kind of proud of you. Go figure." That all made it easier to push her Fiona misgivings aside and think only of Miss Blythe predicting more bravos.

When she got to the arts room that night, she couldn't hear Miss Blythe saying ANYTHING over the chaos that ruled.

The Fruit Loops were grabbing the soccer balls the Wheaties were using in their performance and using them to play keep-away over the heads of the Corn Pops, who were all trying to get their hair buns to look exactly the same. Willoughby's hair was so short and wavy it kept popping out like Slinkies all over her scalp.

Maggie stood in the midst of the Corn Pops, zipping up zippers and adjusting tights.

"They can't even put their pantyhose on right?" Fiona said when Sophie joined her group in the corner.

"They're a bit thick, those four girls are," Darbie said.

Just then Anne-Stuart marched up to Maggie and said her sequined top was itchy, followed by B.J. complaining that her satin shorts made her look fat.

"Those costumes are quite grand," Darbie said. "I don't see what they're raving on about."

"Of course they're grand," Kitty said, tilting her chin up. "Our Maggie made them."

"One thing is for sure," Fiona said. "They are so not going to get a good grade for getting along and being organized. But look at us, all sitting here ready to go."

Sophie glanced over in time to see the victorious gleam still in Fiona's eyes.

Meanwhile, Miss Blythe's hands were punctuating the air with flying exclamation points, and her usually silken hair was looking electrified.

"She's going off her nut," Darbie said.

Kitty giggled. And giggled. And kept giggling until she got the hiccups and had to dart to the restroom before she wet her pants.

"That can't be good," Darbie said.

"Don't worry," Fiona said. "I've got Kitty handled. Besides, she's not freaking out as bad as Willoughby. Look at her."

Willoughby did appear to be losing control. Her head was by now a mass of springs, which were bobbing to and fro as she looked from one scolding Corn Pop to another. They were taking turns putting their noses close to hers and all but chewing her lips off. She finally sat down on the floor, green sequins and all, and bawled like a baby calf.

Miss Blythe did manage to get everyone settled down and explained that they would all sit in the back of the cafeteria during the showcase to watch the other groups perform until it was their group's time to go on. The Corn Flakes grabbed each other's hands and squeezed.

"This is class," Darbie said. "They'll all of them see us, they will."

"See us win," Fiona said.

See us completing our mission, Sophie wanted to say. But Miss Blythe was already swearing them to silence and leading them down the hall toward the cafeteria. Sophie clung to Fiona's hand with her own clammy one and followed.

The cafeteria was festooned with giant shamrocks and green streamers, and every chair was filled with somebody's mom or dad or grandma. Sophie stood on her tiptoes to find Mama and Daddy, who had the video camera in his hand—and Lacie and Zeke, right in front of Boppa's bald head. Fiona's dad was there too, but not her mom, and Sophie felt sad for Fiona—until she spotted another familiar face, twinkling behind wire-rimmed glasses.

"Dr. Peter's here!" she hissed to Fiona.

"No way!"

Sophie tried to point him out, but the lights went off—amid squeals from the sixth-grade class—and Miss Blythe appeared on the stage, hair once again hanging calmly in silky furls. Sophie sucked in a breath she couldn't let go of.

Are we just going to, like, wash everybody's feet when we're doing this? she thought.

Colleen O'Bravo nodded her red ringlets.

Jesus looked at her firmly and kindly.

Sophie LaCroix settled back in her seat and breathed out a long, praying breath.

Most of the groups' presentations were good, especially the Wheaties', who did creative ball passing with feet, heads, and hips, all to music. Even the Fruit Loops were decent, Sophie had to admit. They did a karate demonstration, complete with a lot of loud noises that Fiona whispered weren't necessary. Still, Sophie clapped for them when they took their bows.

And then the Corn Pops performed.

They filled the stage with their green sparkly costumes and glittered hair bows and silver pom-poms and did a routine that was a dance and a cheer and a gymnastics program all kicked and bounced and wiggled into one. Sophie truly thought she was watching something on TV.

Julia could kick her leg so high her foot nearly hit the top of her head.

Anne-Stuart executed one perfect split after another.

B.J.'s cartwheels were as smooth as her satin shorts.

And Willoughby did so many spritely little backflips it made Sophie dizzy.

When they struck their final poses, the whole audience stood up and cheered and whistled and clapped their hands over their heads. Everybody except Fiona.

"It wasn't THAT good," she whispered to Sophie from her seat. "Wait 'til they see ours."

"Come on then," Darbie said, nodding over at Miss Blythe, who was motioning to them from the stage. Sophie could almost see question marks popping out of the teacher's head. "We're on."

It was as if someone had turned a dial in Sophie, making everything go faster than normal speed. They were backstage checking their props and set pieces that Aunt Emily had put in place for them before the show. They were huddled behind the curtain listening to Miss Blythe introduce them with exclamation points in her voice. The lights were on and Kitty was taking a deep breath and marching out onto the stage as if she performed in front of thousands every day. They were starting.

"On a cold March day in 1990," Sophie heard Kitty's voice echo from the microphone, "in the city of Belfast, Northern Ireland—"

And then Darbie was hurrying onto the stage, dressed as her ma and cradling one of Izzy's baby dolls in her arms.

The audience was quiet as Fiona, in her Mr. O'Grady overcoat and hat, swished toward Darbie while Kitty explained about his important work in "the Troubles." Kitty sounded wonderfully serious. Darbie waved to Fiona like a real wife, and Fiona hurried toward her in a husbandly way. Right on Kitty's cue, Sophie held Rory's toy gun above her head backstage and shot it. Fiona crumbled to the ground.

A scattering of chuckles came from the audience.

Sophie froze with her arm still in the air. Across the stage, Darbie looked as if she truly had been shot, before she ran, as she was supposed to, to Fiona/husband and crouched over the body until the lights dimmed and Kitty hurried off to give Fiona the script for her turn.

"They *laughed!*" she whispered as Sophie peeled the coat off Fiona. "It's the Corn Pops and the Fruit Loops."

"They're doing it on purpose, just to mess us up!" Fiona hissed.

Sophie shook her head firmly as she pushed Fiona toward the stage. "We have a mission to accomplish."

"We'll have them in tears in no time," Darbie whispered.

Fiona gave a jerk with her head and went for the microphone. Her voice rang out clear and strong. Sophie put on her Darbie hat and burst into the light.

At first, she couldn't see the faces looking up at her. In fact, it was just like being in a film with only the camera in front of her. Her camera, in Daddy's hands. She broke into a skip as Fiona told about trying to grow up in a place where other children threw rocks at her because she was Catholic. Sophie was Darbie then, and when the crumpled bags were hurled at her, she screamed as if they really were stones, and curled into a ball on the ground.

But once again the audience laughed, from way in the back. They didn't just chuckle this time. There were sure-enough Fruit Loop guffaws and Corn Pop giggles. It was only one loud "SHUSH!" from one of the adults that kept Sophie going, kept her fleeing from the "rocks" that Kitty and Darbie chased her with, disguised in their street-kid caps.

As they frantically grabbed the new set pieces and costumes backstage, Sophie could see that all the girls' eyes were wild.

"Just keep going," she said. "Just do the best you can."

She was proud of them. They did—all of them. In scene after scene they acted their hearts out, being policemen and store owners and rotten kids and the frightened Darbie and her ma. But every time a scene reached its most serious point, the back of the auditorium erupted in harsh snorts and chortles. By the time the Corn Flakes reached the part where Sophie had to kneel at Ma's graveside, she didn't have to try to cry. The tears were already choking up from the hurt place inside her. She and the Corn Flakes had tried so hard.

"It's hard for us to understand," she heard Fiona saying over the microphone, "how it was for Darbie to live with so much fear and sadness. But we have to try, because we can help her start a new life here, and we can become better people ourselves—not always acting heinous because we don't get our way, but thinking about somebody else for a change."

Sophie blinked through her tears. That last line wasn't in the script. Neither was the funny catch in Fiona's voice.

But neither were the giggles that started again in the back of the room.

It definitely wasn't in the script for Sophie to put her face in her hands and cry.

But she did.

Twelve

They didn't get it. *They didn't get it and they never will.*

The thoughts were crying out so loudly in Sophie's head she didn't realize at first that the other roar she was hearing was the audience. But they weren't laughing. They were clapping, in waves that grew stronger and stronger until they were rolling right onto the stage. Somebody was shouting, "Bravo!" and it wasn't Miss Blythe. It sounded like Daddy.

Sophie pulled her face from her hands and looked straight into the eyes of Aunt Emily and Uncle Patrick, and Kitty's mom, and Lacie. Into Daddy's camera lens and Boppa's bald head and Mama's proud face. The whole audience was standing up, and most of the ladies were wiping their eyes.

So was Dr. Peter.

"Take a bow, actors!" Miss Blythe said from the wings. "Get up—take your bows!"

Corn Flakes were suddenly grabbing Sophie from all sides and dragging her to the front of the stage where they bobbed like dashboard dogs and waved. Sophie saw Mama blowing her a kiss and Maggie standing on a chair and grinning a big square grin.

Just before they fled backstage, Sophie also saw the Corn Pops sitting with their arms folded and their eyes rolled. All except

Willoughby, who whistled through her fingers until B.J. reached up and pulled her down by a handful of corkscrew curls.

"I thought the whole audience hated it when there was all that laughing!" Kitty whispered as they made their way through the dark to the backstage steps.

"That was just those Corn Pops, acting the maggot as usual," Darbie said.

Fiona grabbed Sophie by the arm and put her lips close to Sophie's ear. "You don't think it was all the parents just feeling sorry for us, do you?" she whispered.

"No," Sophie whispered back. "I think it was because of what you said. You *got* it, Fiona."

It really didn't matter then, Sophie decided, whether they won a prize or not.

Or at least, not until Miss Blythe swept up onto the stage with three envelopes in her hand. The audience went still, except for the sixth graders, who all sat on the edges of their chairs, tipping them forward and holding Miss Blythe with their eyes. Sophie's heart was slamming in her chest, and she was sure she could hear Fiona's doing the same. She thought she heard Darbie murmuring something about "Jaysus."

Even if we don't win, it's okay, Sophie prayed to him. *But we do deserve to, don't we?*

"Third prize," Miss Blythe said too loudly into the mic, "goes to . . ." She slit the envelope open with a long red fingernail. "The Karate Kids!"

The Fruit Loops whooped like monkeys on Animal Planet, and all of them scrambled up onto the stage and jumped for the envelope.

"Gentlemen," Miss Blythe said, "art is discipline."

The audience laughed one of those aren't-boys-a-mess laughs. Fiona flung her arms around Darbie, Kitty, and Sophie and whispered in a hoarse voice, "The Pops will get second prize and that's okay. We should totally clap for them."

"Of course," Sophie said. "That's what Corn Flakes do."

"We're class," Darbie said.

They squeezed each other tight, and Sophie barely noticed that Kitty was about to cut off the circulation in her left wrist. She held her breath as Miss Blythe produced the second envelope.

"Second prize goes to ..." Slice with the fingernail. Shake out the paper. "The Troubles: Darbie's Story!"

The audience shouted like one person, out-voiced only by the screams of the Corn Pops.

"That means we won!" B.J. shrieked. "We got first!"

"Can our actors come up and receive their prize?" Miss Blythe said.

There was more clapping, and somehow Sophie led the Corn Flakes up to the stage. Kitty bounced like she was on a pogo stick, and Darbie dipped her splashy hair back and forth and smiled shyly as Sophie passed the envelope to her. Her dark eyes were shimmering, and for the first time since Sophie had met her she looked like a real little girl.

But as they all bowed again, Sophie was afraid to look at Fiona. They hadn't won first prize, and it was pretty certain the Pops were going to. Fiona was facing the floor as they bowed so Sophie couldn't see it—though she was surprised Fiona didn't snatch their second prize envelope from Darbie and stomp on it.

They were barely off the stage when the audience buzzed into silence and Miss Blythe cleared her throat into the microphone. "Ladies and gentlemen," she said in a deep voice, "the first-prize winner is the Irish Showdown Dance Troupe!"

The scream Sophie expected from the Corn Pops didn't happen. Instead, while the audience clapped and whistled, they lined up in the back and cartwheeled and backflipped their way up the aisle. In front of the stage, they formed a pyramid topped by Willoughby, who leaped to the stage and started a chain to pull the rest of them up. There they struck a final pose, smiling like a toothpaste commercial.

"Do you think they thought they were going to win?" Fiona said to Sophie beneath the roar of the audience.

Sophie searched her face. Fiona was smiling and shaking her head, even as she clapped.

"Too bad they aren't class," Fiona said. She hooked her arm through Darbie's. "But we know who is."

Wow, Sophie thought *Just — wow.*

Melting with happy relief, she latched onto Kitty with one hand and waved Maggie over with the other. The Corn Pops hadn't bothered to invite her onto the stage, and Maggie looked like she'd rather be standing with her Corn Flakes anyway. Maggie got to them just in time to smile at Daddy, who had his back turned to the stage completely and was filming Sophie and the girls with a victory grin on his face. He usually only looked like that when the Dallas Cowboys won.

There were shamrock-shaped cookies and green punch and certificates for all the participants after the show. The Corn Flakes gathered around Darbie to see what the prize in the envelope was.

"A boat tour of the Chesapeake Bay!" Darbie read.

"Just as long as somebody else is steering," Fiona said.

They grinned at each other.

Once Sophie hugged her family and Boppa and Aunt Emily, she skipped the food and went in search of Dr. Peter. He was hanging out near the punch bowl wearing his enormous green top hat.

"Sophie, me lass!" he said when he saw her. And then he dropped his Irish accent, and his eyes grew soft.

"Did you like it—was it okay?" Sophie said.

"Oh, Loodle," he said. "It was fabulous—and you know I would never lie to you. I'm so proud of you."

"I messed up a little. I wasn't supposed to cry that much at the end."

"Why not? The rest of us did." He cocked his head at her. "You weren't acting then, were you?"

"No," Sophie said. The second prize and the bravos were fizzling out of her. "I was crying because they were laughing. I guess the Corn Pops and the Fruit Loops really are that hateful."

"You think they were laughing to make you look bad?" Dr. Peter said. "It didn't work, did it?"

Sophie shook her head. She felt like she was going to cry again.

"Okay, Loodle, dish. What's going on?"

Sophie looked over her shoulder. "We're having a session right here?"

"No, this is just two friends talking about why you feel bad."

"Because our mission—it failed. We wanted everybody to understand about Darbie and how hard her life was and how there are more important things than being popular and winning and stuff. Fiona got it—right while she was up on the stage—but none of the other kids did, and they were the ones we were doing it for. They were the feet we were trying to wash." Sophie smacked at a tear with her fingers. "I just wanted them to understand."

Dr. Peter leaned down, almost covering Sophie with the brim of his hat. "I'll let you in on a little secret," he said. "I think they understood very clearly. They saw themselves up there in those kids that threw rocks and shouted mean things, and they were embarrassed. That's why they laughed."

"No offense, Dr. Peter," Sophie said. "But Corn Pops and Fruit Loops don't get embarrassed."

"Not for long, but they do have that 'oops' feeling for a bit of a moment before they cover it up. Just look over there."

Dr. Peter winked, just like a leprechaun, Sophie thought, and nodded his hat toward the stage. There were the Corn Pops, still in costume, flipping and splitting and backflipping, and completing each move with outstretched arms and a dazzling smile — like they were going for gold at the Olympics. It made Sophie feel itchy. There was performing, and then there was just plain old showing off.

For a minute Sophie thought Dr. Peter was wrong. None of them looked the least bit embarrassed about the fact that they were doing an encore that nobody was watching. Until Sophie saw a wavy-haired person slip off the front edge of the stage and look back, cheeks blotchy-red and shoulders curving almost to meet at her chest. Willoughby shook out what had survived of her bun, folded her arms across the front of her sequined top, and walked stiffly away. Behind her, the Pops gathered for a pyramid and B.J. yelled, "Hey, where's Willoughby?"

Willoughby gave a nervous laugh and disappeared into the crowd of parents.

"Embarrassed by her own kind," Dr. Peter said. "And what did she do?"

"She laughed," Sophie said. "But by Monday she'll be hanging out with them again."

"Not unless somebody else gets to her first." Dr. Peter gave her another leprechaun wink and said, "Happy St. Patty's Day, Loodle. I'll see you soon in my office. Looks like we'll have a lot to talk about."

And then with a twinkle, he was gone too.

Sophie stood there for a minute watching the Fruit Loops tearing down the streamers with karate chops and the Corn Pops showing off for no one and her own Corn Flakes introducing Darbie to their families.

There would be a lot to tell Jesus tonight when it was quiet and she could imagine him washing her feet. They were pretty tired feet. Acting was hard work.

She would tell him that she and the Flakes had shown all the love they could, maybe some to the Pops even if they didn't get it. She'd also tell him that Fiona understood finally—and Kitty—and probably Maggie. Maybe even Lacie.

And possibly somebody else who could now use a foot washing. Maybe not right away. Perhaps just an invitation to sit at their lunch table would be good first, and then a part in their upcoming film about Colleen O'Bravo.

Sophie smiled to herself. *What a class idea*, she thought.

And she went off to look for Willoughby.

Glossary

barnacled (bar-nah-KULD) when something is covered in icky sea creatures that look like little rocks or shells

bevy (bev-EE) a word used to describe the number of people that gather in one place

catastrophe (ka-tas-truh-FEE) a complete disaster, usually one that isn't easy to fix

chaperone (sha-PURR-own) an adult or person in authority who acts as a fancy babysitter

coalition (co-uh-LI-shun) a bunch of people who join together and try to change something they think is wrong

desperate (des-PER-ate) (1) When something really needs to be fixed up, or someone really needs help; (2) feeling panicked when you don't have any other choices

devastation (dev-ahs-TA-shun) when everything is falling apart and in ruins, usually because something really bad happened

diabolical (die-ah-BOLL-eh-call) a completely evil action, or at least a really terrible thing to do

disdainful (dis-DANE-full) acting like a spoiled princess and looking down on someone because you think they're acting like an idiot

guffaw (guf-FAWW) when you find something really funny, and can't help but laugh really loud

insatiably (in-SAY-shuh-blee) the state of never being completely satisfied, and always wanting to know more

nonsensical (non-SEN-si-cull) doing something so silly it defies logic

obnoxious (ob-KNOCK-shus) a person who is offensive and a complete pain in the bum, and who drives everyone crazy

pantomime (pan-TOW-mime) acting out a story without a script, using only a narrator and your body expressions to tell the story

plethora (PLETH-er-a) a general term used to describe a lot of something, like when there's almost too much

sacred (SAY-crid) something that's holy and should be treated with special care

Tasmanian devil (taz-main-E-an DEV-ill) a mean little animal that lives in Australia and looks like an overgrown rat. It's also the name of a cartoon character that has *way* too much energy.

tousled (TUH-silled) something, usually hair, that was blown about and becomes a tangled mess

usurping (you-SIRP-ing) basically, to steal something away from someone by using a lot of force to get it

SOPHIE'S
First Dance

Book 5
Bonus Chapter

One

Are you going to feed us something weird for your report?"

Sophie LaCroix looked up from the library table into the disdainful face of B.J. Schneider. *Disdainful* was a word Sophie's best friend, Fiona, had taught her, and this word definitely worked when B.J. or one of the other Corn Pops narrowed her eyes into slits, curled her lip, and acted as if Sophie were barely worth the breath it was taking to say something heinous to her.

"As a matter of fact, yes," that same Fiona said as she tucked a strand of dark hair behind her ear. It popped back out and draped over one gray eye. "We thought we'd dish up some sautéed roaches on a bed of seaweed with a nice snake venom sauce."

Sophie dragged a piece of her own hair under her nose like a mustache.

"It is so disgusting when you do that," said another Corn Pop, Anne-Stuart—with the usual juicy sniff up her nostrils.

Not as disgusting as you and your sinus problems, Sophie thought. But she didn't say it. All of the Corn Flakes had taken a vow not to be hateful to the Corn Pops ever, no matter how heinous THEY were to the Flakes.

B.J. put her hands on her slightly pudgy hips. "I KNOW you aren't really going to serve something that nasty for your culture project," she said.

Fiona pulled her bow of a mouth into a sly smile. "Then why did you ask?"

B.J. and Anne-Stuart rolled their eyes with the precision of synchronized swimmers.

"What are y'all doing for your presentation?" Sophie said, adjusting her glasses on her nose.

"We AND Julia and Willoughby—we're doing a folk dance," Anne-Stuart said. "And we're going to make the whole class participate."

"You're going to 'make' us?" Fiona said.

Sophie cleared her throat. Sometimes Fiona had a little trouble keeping the vow. It *was* hard with the Corn Pops acting like they ran Great Marsh Elementary, especially when school stretched into Saturdays at the town library.

"Then everybody can get used to dancing with each other," Anne-Stuart said. She sniffled. "That way, SOME people won't feel so lame at the graduation dance."

"What graduation dance?" Sophie and Fiona said together. Sophie's voice squeaked higher than Fiona's, which brought a heavy-eyebrowed look from the librarian.

"What dance?" Fiona said again.

B.J. and Anne-Stuart both sat down at the table with Sophie and Fiona—as if they'd been invited—and B.J. shoved aside the *Food from Around the World* book they'd been looking at while Anne-Stuart leaned in her long, lean frame. Sophie was sure she could see moisture glistening on Anne-Stuart's nose hairs.

"The dance the school is having at the end of the year for our sixth-grade graduation," she said.

"Duh," B.J. put in.

"Who decided that?" Fiona said.

"Just the entire class. Back in September." B.J. gave her buttery-blonde bob a toss. "You were probably off in one of those weird things y'all do—making up stories—"

"No," Fiona said. "I wasn't even HERE yet in September. I moved here in October."

"I know YOU were here," Anne-Stuart said, pointing at Sophie.

Sophie shrugged. She knew she had probably daydreamed her way through the entire voting process. That was back before she'd gotten her video camera, and before she and the Corn Flakes had started making films out of their daydreams instead of getting in trouble for having them in school and missing important things like voting for a stupid dance.

"What were the other choices?" Fiona said.

"Who cares?" B.J. said. "We're having a dance, and everybody's going to wear, like, dress-up clothes, and—"

"So if you didn't even know about the dance," Anne-Stuart said, "then you obviously don't have your dates yet."

"Dates?" Sophie said.

"You mean, as in boys?" Fiona said.

Anne-Stuart snorted and covered her mouth. B.J. waved at the librarian, whose eyebrows were now up in her hairline.

"You know," Anne-Stuart whispered. "Boys. The ones with the cute legs."

"Cute LEGS?" Sophie's voice squeaked out of her own nostrils, and she was sure Anne-Stuart was going to drip right out of her chair. B.J. kept smiling at the librarian.

"People are actually coming to the dance with DATES?" Fiona said.

"You meet your date at the dance, and he doesn't dance with anybody else but you the whole night." Anne-Stuart put her hand on Fiona's and wrinkled her forehead. "You don't HAVE to. I mean, if you can't get a boy to be with you, then you can't."

"I don't WANT a boy to be with me, thank you very much," Fiona said. She snatched back her hand.

Sophie was doing the mustache thing with her hair again. What boy in their class would she even want to get within three feet of? One of the Fruit Loops — Tod or Eddie or Colton? The thought made her feel like she had the stomach flu coming on. She shrank her already tiny form down into the chair.

Tod Ravelli had a pointy face like a Dr. Seuss character and acted like he was all big, even though he was one of the shrimpiest boys in the class. Acting big included trying to make Sophie feel like a worm.

Colton Messik wasn't any better. He seemed to think he was cute the way he could make the Corn Pops squeal when he told a joke. Sophie and the rest of the Flakes thought the only thing funny about him was the way his ears stuck out.

And Eddie Wornom was the worst. He acted like Mr. Football, but mostly he was what Sophie's mom called "fluffy" around the tummy, and he was louder than the other two put together, especially when he was calling their friend Maggie "Maggot" or some other lovely thing.

"I doubt any boy would ask you anyway," B.J was saying to Fiona. "Not unless it was one of the computer geeks. Vincent or one of the boy-twins or — I know! Jimmy Wythe — he's like the KING of the computer geeks. You could go with him."

Fiona let her head fall to the side, closed her eyes, and pretended to snore. Sophie watched the librarian march toward them. B.J. lowered her voice. "But you'd better hurry up because there are more girls than boys in our class. You COULD get left out."

"We have to go," Anne-Stuart said. She grabbed B.J.'s hand, pulling her from the chair, and cocked her head at Mrs. Eyebrows. Silky-blonde tresses spilled along the side of Anne-Stuart's face.

"We tried to get them to be quiet, ma'am," she said. She and B.J. trailed off.

"Come on," Fiona said. "Let's wait for Kitty and those guys outside."

Sophie left *Food from Around the World* on the table and followed Fiona past the glowering Mrs. Eyebrows and on outside — where a corridor of trees sheltered the library and Poquoson, Virginia's City Hall from the road. Big, fluffy hydrangea bushes provided a getaway spot for the two of them. Sophie sat down on the curb and wriggled herself under a snowball cluster of blue flowers with Fiona perched next to her.

"Just when I think they couldn't GET any more scornful, they reveal yet another layer of contempt — " Fiona's eyes narrowed, Corn Pop style. "They're evil."

Sophie nodded. "And Julia wasn't even with them. Or Willoughby."

"Julia always lets them do the dirty work, being the queen and all. And Willoughby — you can hardly tell if she's even a Corn Pop anymore. Have you noticed that sometimes she's with them and sometimes she's not?"

"I invited her to hang out with us that one time — "

"And the Pops snatched her right back. Even if THEY don't want to be her friends, they don't want US to be her friends. I told you — they're evil."

Sophie squirmed. "What about this dance thing?"

"It's lame. I vote the Corn Flakes just don't even go. We have better things to do. Hey — I have an idea." Fiona nodded toward Sophie's backpack. "Get your camera out. Let's hide in this bush and film Kitty and Darbie and Maggie when they get here."

Sophie felt a grin spreading across her face. "Let's pretend we're secret agents—"

"Hired to do surveillance on—"

"A new group of agents being gathered for a special mission—"

"Quick—here comes Maggie's mom's car!"

As Senora LaQuita's big old Pontiac pulled into the parking lot, Sophie climbed into the hydrangea bush with Fiona, fished the camera out of her backpack, and became—

Agent Shadow. With a practiced hand—and eye—Agent Shadow framed her fellow agent in the lens. Wide-set brown eyes, dark chin-length hair, and a classic jaw line revealed her Latino heritage. An experienced agent knew these things. The dark-haired agent didn't say goodbye as she drew her boxy-square frame from the car, but, then, according to classified information, this was not a smiley spy. Agent-from-Cuba was known as the most serious of this collection of agents from all over the world.

Yeah—an international group. That was good, Sophie decided.

As Maggie plodded up the library walk with her leather backpack, Sophie panned the camera, but Fiona gave her a poke and pointed back to the parking lot. A van was pulling up.

"There's Kitty," Sophie whispered to Fiona.

Agent Shadow focused the camera and watched the girl hop down from the van, her black ponytail bouncing. Agent Shadow continued to film Agent Ponytail as she stood on tiptoe to talk through the window to the driver. Agent Shadow was sure Ponytail was getting ALL the instructions about when to be back at headquarters—for the fourth time at least. This agent's documents had revealed that she could be scatterbrained at times. Just as Ponytail turned, Agent Shadow got a good shot of her profile—an upturned nose that looked like it had been chiseled out of china. Agent Ponytail was very un-agent-like. That must be part of her cover.

"Hey, Mags!" Kitty called up the walk.

Agent Shadow jumped and collided with Agent Big Words, nearly tumbling the two of them from their hiding place—

"Better let me," Fiona said. She picked up the camera from where it teetered on a hydrangea branch.

Agent Shadow grew more intent as she crept deeper under cover. She had been in the field for forty-eight straight hours without sleep. Perhaps it was time to let Agent Big Words take over the filming.

She watched, her mind razor-sharp, as Agent Ponytail hugged the neck of Agent-from-Cuba. Agent Ponytail appeared to be the slobbery type. Agent-from-Cuba obviously was not.

"Psst—here comes Darbie!" Fiona hissed.

Agent Shadow swiveled her gaze to the figure getting out of a BMW. She was the newest agent to be recruited into this gathering. Recently arriving from Northern Ireland, she would have much to add to the mission internationally speaking, especially when Agent Shadow determined just what the mission was—which would come later. It always came later.

Refreshed from her short break from the camera, Agent Shadow snatched it back from Agent Big Words and zoomed in on the subject striding up the walk. She was swinging her arms and her reddish hair and taking in everything with flashing black eyes.

"Agent Irish will be helpful in giving each of our agents new names and identities," Agent Shadow told herself. "Once we figure out what dangerous, risky, and utterly vital mission we'll be on. But first I must see just how observant she is. Can we remain hidden—or is she just as sharp as her file says she is?"

Even though Agent Shadow burrowed herself deeper into the treacherous tangle of brush, she could see Agent Irish growing bigger in her lens — and bigger — and bigger —

"Don't be thinking you're sly, you two," Darbie said, her nose pressed against the camera lens. "You're just a bit obvious."

"But we got you on film!" Fiona said. She crawled from behind the bush, shaking tiny blue blossoms from her hair. Sophie wriggled out after her.

"Our next Corn Flakes production should be a spy film, I think," Sophie said.

"My mom could make us trench coats," Maggie said.

Fiona bunched up her lips. "That's better than dance dresses."

"DANCE dresses?" Kitty's clear blue eyes were lighting up like tiny flames. "That's right — the sixth-grade dance!"

"You knew about it?" Fiona said.

"Of course she did. So did I." Maggie shrugged. "They do it every year."

Darbie gave a grunt. "You won't be seeing me at a dance. Those Corn Pops already made me feel like an eejit about my dancing when I first came here." *Eejit* was *idiot* in Darbie's Northern Irish accent. It was one of her favorite words. "I'd rather be making a spy flick," she said.

"Exactly," Fiona said.

Sophie looked at Kitty, who was poking at a weed growing up through a walkway crack with the toe of her pink flip-flop.

"You WANT to go to the dance, Kitty?" Sophie said.

"Kind of," Kitty said. "It would be fun to be all, like, dressed up. We don't HAVE to dance." Kitty's voice was starting to spiral up into a whine. Whining was one of the things she did best.

"You just want to get dressed up and go stand around?" Fiona said.

"Maybe we could just dance with each another—"

"And pretend we're agents in disguise, keeping the Corn Pop organization in our sights," Sophie said.

"That definitely has possibilities," Fiona said, rubbing her chin. "What if we could foil their plans with their 'dates'?"

"Define 'foil'" Darbie said.

"I think that means mess them up," Sophie said.

Darbie giggled. "You mean, like mix them up so they end up dancing with each other's boyfriends?" she said.

"The only thing is," Sophie said, "we can't be hateful to the Pops just because they're hateful to us. Corn Flake code."

"I know—bummer," Fiona said. She sighed. "But you're right. We'll have to think of some other mission."

"Whatever it is, we can't let them see us filming them," Darbie put in.

"WE don't have to dance with any boys though, do we?" Maggie's voice was thudding even harder than usual.

"Absolutely not," Darbie said. "We'll have nothing to do with those blaggards."

Blaggards, Sophie thought, repeating the word *blackguards* in her mind the way Darbie had pronounced it. With her Irish accent, Darbie could make anything sound exciting and exotic and worth doing.

"We might look a little suspicious not dancing with ANY boys," Kitty said. "It's not like ALL of them are blackguards."

"The Fruit Loops definitely are," Fiona said with a sniff. She dropped down on the grass and the rest of the Corn Flakes joined her.

Darbie nodded slowly. "But those boys that are always raving on about computers—they aren't THAT bad."

"You mean like Nathan and Vincent and Jimmy and the twins?" Sophie said.

"Ross and Ian," Kitty said.

Sophie peered at Kitty through her glasses. Kitty was looking suspiciously dreamy, and Sophie had a feeling it wasn't about being a secret agent.

"I can't keep any of them straight," Darbie said.

"Nathan's way skinny and he got first place in the science fair, remember?" Kitty said.

"No," Fiona said. "Why do you remember?"

Kitty's cheeks got pink. "His dad's in my dad's squadron. I see him at picnics and stuff."

"Carry on," Darbie said, pointing at Kitty with a piece of grass.

"Like I said, Ross and Ian are the twins—"

"Round faces," Maggie said.

"Not Eddie Wornom-round, though," Sophie said.

"No—eew," Kitty said. "What else, Darbie?" Her eyes were shining, and Sophie could tell she was enjoying this role.

This might come in handy when we make our secret agent movie, Sophie thought. She was already thinking of plot twists that could make use of Agent Ponytail's powers of observation.

"Vincent—which one is he?"

"Curly hair, braces," Fiona said.

"And he has kind of a deep voice," Kitty cut in—before Fiona could take her job away from her, Sophie thought. "Only it goes high sometimes."

"I know exactly who he is," Darbie said. "He isn't as much of an eejit as a lot of them."

"You left out Jimmy Wythe," Maggie said matter-of-factly.

Kitty shrugged. "I don't know that much about him. He's quiet." She gave a soft giggle. "That kind of makes him mysterious."

"Or a geek," Fiona said.

"Okay," Sophie said. "So when we come up with a mission, if we have to dance with any boys it'll be just those not-mean ones. Is everybody in?"

Fiona stuck out her pinky finger, and Kitty latched onto it. Maggie hooked onto Kitty's, and Sophie crooked her pinky around Maggie's. Only Darbie was left.

"Are we promising there will be no dates for us though?" she said.

"Not a chance," Fiona said.

Darbie gave a serious nod, and then she curved one pinky around Sophie's and the other around Fiona's.

"It's a Corn Flakes pact then," Fiona said. "No one breaks it."

"We better get to work on our culture project now," Maggie said.

Kitty giggled and hiked herself up onto Maggie's back, right on top of her backpack. "Can't we talk about our dresses first?" she said.

"Costumes," Sophie said. "For the film."

As the Corn Flakes meandered toward the library door, Sophie held back. She had a feeling this was going to be the Corn Flakes' most important movie yet—and maybe even Agent Shadow's most important mission. It was going to take some serious dreaming to get it just right.

And as she watched her fellow agents disappear into the agency building, Agent Shadow glanced back over both shoulders to be sure there was no one from the Corn Pop Organization spying on them even now. An agent could never be too careful.

Sophie Series
Written by Nancy Rue

Meet Sophie LaCroix, a creative soul who's destined to become a great film director someday. But many times her overactive imagination gets her in trouble!

Check out the other books in the series!

Book 1: Sophie's World
IBSN: 978-0-310-70756-1

Book 2: Sophie's Secret
ISBN: 978-0-310-70757-8

Book 3: Sophie Under Pressure
ISBN: 978-0-310-71840-6

Book 4: Sophie Steps Up
ISBN: 978-0-310-71841-3

Book 5: Sophie's First Dance
ISBN: 978-0-310-70760-8

Book 6: Sophie's Stormy Summer
ISBN: 978-0-310-70761-5

Book 7: Sophie's Friendship Fiasco
ISBN: 978-0-310-71842-0

Book 8: Sophie and the New Girl
ISBN: 978-0-310-71843-7

Book 9: Sophie Flakes Out
ISBN: 978-0-310-71024-0

Book 10: Sophie Loves Jimmy
ISBN: 978-0-310-71025-7

Book 11: Sophie's Drama
ISBN: 978-0-310-71844-4

Book 12: Sophie Gets Real
ISBN: 978-0-310-71845-1

We want to hear from you. Please send your comments
about this book to us in care of zreview@zondervan.com. Thank you.

ZONDERVAN.com/
AUTHORTRACKER
follow your favorite authors